Without
Waking
Up

Without Waking Up

CAROLINA SCHUTTI

Translated by Deirdre McMahon

bullaun press

First published 2023 by

BULLAUN PRESS
Sligo, Ireland
www.bullaunpress.com

10 9 8 7 6 5 4 3 2 1
Originally published in German as *einmal muss ich über weiches Gras gelaufen sein* by OTTO MÜLLER VERLAG, 2012

ISBN 978 1 7398423 2 1

Bullaun Press gratefully acknowledges the financial support of the Arts Council / An Chomhairle Ealaíon.

Set in 10.5 over 16 pt Sabon by Niall McCormack
Printed in Dublin by SprintPrint

To my grandmothers

I
Babushka

Just begin, Maja said, so many first sentences.

She's not called Babushka, she's Matryoshka, said my great-aunt, my father's only aunt, even though she didn't know any Russian. Although she was right, I just did not believe her. I had always called mine Babushka, shaken her carefully, taken her apart and put her together again, examining the smallest one very carefully to see if there was a hidden mechanism to let me open her like the others; I could not believe I had reached the last one.

I would often lie awake letting my eyes wander around the room and I would tell the biggest Babushka what the house looked like from the outside: about the garden, sprawling outwards, the shade that lay over most of the houses for more than half the year. I would tell her about the valley with its wooded hillsides, about the night sky stretching tightly over it. It frightened me that no one could tell me what lay behind it. But perhaps you just needed to ask the right questions to get an answer. The Babushka would look at me with her big eyes and I would open her up, take the smallest doll out, lay her tenderly in my hand, rocking her to and fro, amazed at how grown up she looked.

My Babushka had gone missing, or so they led me to believe, but that was impossible. I had never taken her outside. Perhaps my aunt decided that I was too big for dolls and hid her in the attic or threw her away. Maybe she had found the nightly murmuring from my room disturbing. I never asked.

I told Marek about Babushka and he stroked the hair behind my ears and kissed me on the forehead.

Moje kochanie, he whispered, and I knew what that meant even though I knew no Polish and had lost the Belarusian of my first years, along with Babushka.

Marek had a little wooden house with an unkempt garden. He offered old Walter money for gardening, but Walter did little more than get rid of a few branches. He said mowing was impossible because there were too many scrubby bushes along the fence and around the house. He left the bushes as they were and bought himself schnapps.

Marek didn't drink schnapps; he never drank. Nevertheless, his eyes were sometimes red when he sat at the window looking out.

They hadn't died one after the other, as local gossip suggested. Marek once told me that his uncle went first, then his grandmother. Then Micha, his favourite nephew, died. He hung himself from a tree, from the tree that his grandfather had planted for the uncle. He didn't speak about his mother and father. Everyone knew what had happened, but nobody could explain why Marek had moved to this particular village as a young man and why he hadn't returned home after the war.

Forget all that now, Marek had said, wiping his eyes, forget it. However, I never forgot, and I asked my aunt if she could tell me anything about Marek. The shady side is bad, she answered, going on to ask me why that was any of my business. I asked why there were houses here anyway when the shady side is so bad, but I got no answer.

The snow arrived early and stayed a long time. Even at the height of summer you needed a woollen jacket by four in the afternoon if you wanted to play outside. Only mint and chamomile, dill and garlic grew in the garden. When you ran barefoot on the grass it prickled the soles of your feet. I just could not imagine soft grass, or not anymore. As a small child I must have run over soft grass, at least once. Years later my aunt gave me a photo showing my mother and me in a park. I was wearing a short little white dress embroidered with flowers, with a hand-crocheted border on the collar. My mother was holding my hand, laughing at the camera, not staying still for the photo; her arm and face were out of focus. We were standing barefoot on the grass, and I looked uncertain. My eyes were wide open, my lips an open slit.

My aunt didn't want me to visit Marek. She thought I'd be better off playing with other children. I often acted as if I had spent the whole afternoon playing tag and French skipping. I would kneel in the meadow on the way home and stroke the palm of my hand over damp earth. Sometimes, if I had enough time, I would lie down in the grass and look up at the clouds as they took on a rosy-red tinge and when the light was fading, I could observe the countless tiny insects who crowded the skies and made the air restless.

It was not that I wanted to turn myself into an insect and flee from there; I hadn't thought that far ahead. And I didn't want to be an animal either, though having a favourite animal and knowing everything about it came with the territory back then. After school Fini asked me what kind of animal I would like to be, continuing in the same breath to say that I didn't need to answer as she already knew, definitely a bird – or an angel so that I could follow my mother to heaven. I didn't want to fly to my mother because it was cramped and cold beneath the earth or so my aunt had told me, and I believed her.

There are various Babushkas. Some resemble each other down to the finest details and some have different pictures on their fronts. A different picture on every front and you know immediately which story belongs to it. And the big Babushka holds all the stories together like the cover of a book of fairy tales. You need to study the smallest picture especially carefully because if you are lucky, even this tiny surface has a background showing a forest or a stream or flowers. I was lucky. My Babushka was particularly beautiful. I can remember every picture and I still know the stories that went with the pictures; they translated themselves without me noticing.

Marek often asked me to tell him these stories. I thought that maybe they reminded him of the stories of his childhood, because they were similar, but perhaps he only wanted to prevent them fading from my memory.

Marek would give me presents of sweets or colourful stones which I would store under a loose board in my room. Whenever I was out with my aunt and we met him by chance, he would just give us a curt hello, hardly looking at me, as if he were indifferent towards me. But in the afternoons when I went to his house, he would stroke my cheeks and sit down opposite me at the heavy wooden table, drinking black tea with milk and sugar from a glass printed with flowers. Because of me, he always had a choice of drinks in his larder that I never got otherwise. I loved the sparkling yellow or red drinks. I would sit on Marek's lap letting him read books aloud or tell me stories, hanging on his every word. There was an unevenness about his voice that only I could hear, or so I thought back then, something in his tone that reminded me of something from the past, from way back in my early days.

When I got big enough to take the bus into the next town my aunt would send me shopping once a week. She gave me two cloth bags and, for weeks, she would make me recite the bus stops and the departure times before I left the house. I never forgot anything and occasionally I was allowed to buy something small for myself. As time went on, I got to know all the shops and became much quicker at completing my errands, so I had time to wander the streets and look at the shop windows. That was when I began to think about my mother more often. I would stand in front of the shop windows trying to superimpose my reflection onto the clothes on display. Sometimes it worked but in other shops the clothes were hanging just too high. I imagined what it would be like to have my mother's face reflected beside mine, how beside her I could smile at the displays and we would hold each other's hands.

Sometimes I asked myself what it would be like to hold a young man's hand, to go with him, as Fini called it. I tried to walk tall as I wandered up and down the street. According to Fini, pulling in my tummy was really important, like wiggling my hips so that it looked like I was wearing high heels. I used to imagine what would happen if a young man brought me over to the sunny side of the street. He would ask my mother if she would allow him to take her beloved only daughter away – yes, that was just what he would say – and my mother would smile and nod, catch me by the shoulder and nudge me towards the young man, folding her hands across her chest, waiting until he had given me a kiss and taken me in his arms. And then she would wave until we had vanished around a corner.

Fini sometimes took me by the hand when we were wandering through the woods. If it got dark on the way home, she would clutch me so tightly that the prints of her fingers were visible on my hands for a long time afterwards. I never told her that she was hurting me. On long summer afternoons when we had had enough of other people's company and I wasn't with Marek, we would sit down at the stream, dangling our feet in the water until they turned red. Then we would lie down on the flat sun-warmed banks and pull up our shirts to tan our tummies. Fini told me stories, not fairy tales. She would tell me what she knew about the other girls and their families, about her older brother and his friends and girlfriends and plenty about what she had observed through keyholes. She explained what it would be like in a couple of years when we became young women, and men would be interested in our tanned legs and torsos. I loved listening to her as her sentences flowed on like the stream, almost a calming murmur and, although there were no ogres like Baba Jaga and bewitched kings' daughters, I hung on her every word. Her family would become mine for an afternoon. I used to take Fini's stories home with me, feeling that I had experienced something and escaped out of the shadows. One evening I wrote a sentence, a phrase that had struck me on the way home: if only a person could keep all these stories like a protective shield in front of their body, wrapping strange sentences around them like a camouflage coat. I read the sentence aloud to Fini the next time we met but she just looked down on me and started laughing. I crumpled up the paper, put it away and threw it in the stream on the way home, knowing that it would soon become tiny scraps, dissolving completely in the cold water. Such a sentence never struck me again and I would never again write anything like that. But I remember this sentence.

You just have to start over again every time, said my aunt when I gathered my courage and asked her about before, although I felt that she wouldn't answer this time either, and would make me feel my question had embarrassed her. The past I had experienced with my mother collided with the past I had with my aunt; I had no idea of where their edges touched, no memory of how I had come out of the city to the village.

To this day I know I didn't understand my aunt. She talked at me in an unfamiliar language, and I was supposed to say 'Papa' to the strange man who had collected me. At first, I saw him only at weekends and then less and less because he took my aunt's advice to heart and made a new beginning. I was allowed to stay with my aunt; she was glad of company in the over-large house.

Here wasn't good enough for your mother, my aunt said, she left the village and your father behind when you were just a few weeks old, but she didn't want a divorce, and to this day my aunt didn't know why.

And now that you are here, be content. I knew I had to be content.

When Marek died, I no longer lived in the village. The photo on his death notice shows him as a fifty-year-old; I know this for certain because that had been his nicest birthday, because that photo stood on a narrow shelf beside the house door, his best birthday, he used to say in any case. Fifty-fifty, someone had written on the lower edge in white touch-up pen. His life had not lasted a hundred years, but who can say how much life a person gets. My aunt died before him. She reached the age of eighty-three and nobody needs to worry about her grave. She had ordered and paid for a headstone herself years before her death and anyone who wants to can place a candle on her grave or lay a bunch of flowers to be dried by the sun and blown away by the wind. She knew I would never come back.

I did not come back; I couldn't. I got a Matryoshka that looks so like my old one, my hidden or thrown away Matryoshka. I took it apart and set all the dolls out in a row. There are scenes from fairy tales on the dolls' fronts, but now they make me sad when I remember them. I lost my language along with my mother: the falling-asleep phrases, the comforting phrases, this cradle-rocking of words, our language island where there was just enough room for the two of us, on which we wandered through the city to the playground or the bakery. Latrine, shovel, and bread roll – I can't remember what German words I had when I came to my aunt's. And now: encouraging phrases from the dictionary, encouraging sentences spoken on tape but the lullaby does not want to return, and those sentences remain forgotten.

Moj bednyj anjol, my mother must have said, *moj bednyi anjol*.

I turn the dolls around and let them look out the window. From behind, they all look the same – light blue flowers on a red background. Where are my first sentences, I ask myself – I only ask now that I have grown into a complete language for a few years and withered again on the shady side – they're not even in memory, at least not in mine.

II
A Feathery Cave

Don't just stand in the doorway, says her aunt.

Maja pushes herself away from the doorframe, taking a step forwards, towards her aunt.

Has it arrived? asks Maja.

Her aunt dries her wet hands on the tea towel, takes her knitted jacket down from the hook, slips into the right sleeve first, then the left; she always does the right side first, closes two buttons, then rolls up her sleeves and turns back to the sink. Maja gives her aunt a sideways glance, and without a word, takes a tea towel and helps with the drying. The delicate Sunday china, white porcelain with a light-blue pattern, the freshly dried plates and cups belong beneath the others in the cupboard. Maja climbs onto a chair; her aunt holds up four plates and Maja inserts two plates together under the stack. Her aunt has taught her this so that all the dishes are used in rotation. She can manage the cups on her own and her aunt has already put the glasses on their own shelf. Then comes the cutlery.

Be careful, says her aunt, the knife is sharp. She says that every time and Maja grasps it by the handle and dries the blade carefully. When her aunt isn't looking, she runs her finger cautiously along the blade before returning it to the kitchen drawer. The heavy pans are the only things that make her nervous and she needs both hands to carry them to the table, drying the inside first, then turning them upside down to dry the base and handles. She leaves them on the table and her aunt hangs them up on the hooks; the sound as they strike the thick stone wall breaks the hour of silence: they don't talk during meals, and they are too busy taking care not to break anything while they are washing up – talking is a distraction anyway, people talk too much, her aunt says. Maja hangs the tea towel on the back of a chair to dry. Her aunt pulls the sleeves of her jacket down to cover her wrists and rubs her reddened hands together.

Has it arrived? Maja asks again and her aunt gives her a quick look and shakes her head. It's Sunday and there's no post on Sundays and nothing will come now; Easter was three weeks ago. Her aunt shoos Maja out of the kitchen, opens one of the little windows and closes the door behind her.

The child has got big, she thinks, three years is no time for an old woman and an eternity for a child. How it seems like yesterday that her father was going in and out of here – she brought him up because his mother did not want him – how he has to live his life without this child who arrived here all at once, a child who looked so like his wife, about whom he never spoke again.

Maja stands in the doorway observing her aunt as she ties her shoelaces carefully, then throws a fleeting glance in the mirror hanging high on the wall.

I'll be back in two hours, she says, don't get up to any mischief.

Maja goes into the parlour, the wooden floor creaks under the striped rugs. Maja knows exactly where to walk to make them creak loudest. She takes the loud path, stamping with all her weight on the boards. Nobody scolds her and she walks back the same way, then along the wall to the seat of the tiled stove. She kneels up on it; there are always flowers on the wide windowsills, even in winter. Maja plucks a couple of withered flowers and lays them in a row along the sill, then props her chin in her hands and looks out. There is nothing to see. Clouds, a grass-covered hill, a garden fence, a strip of the neighbouring house, part of a barn. A straw cross from Palm Sunday is stuck just under the barn roof with a red-white-red striped ribbon hanging limply from it.

Why had her father not written, neither for Christmas, nor for Easter; at other times his cards had arrived punctually, sometimes a week or two early.

My Dears, Happy Christmas or Happy Easter.

Her aunt would always read the brief greeting aloud and then place the card in a box with the others. Whenever Maja wanted to know if there was anything more on the card her aunt would shake her head and once, when she asked why her father wasn't there anymore, why he never visited and where he was living, she told Maja to look to the future, watching her as she spoke, so Maja bit her lip until her aunt turned around and left the room.

You can't cut yourself a slice of the past, she often says. Her aunt is an expert at cutting: she cuts bread, onions, bacon, carrots, tomatoes. She cooks with enamel pots, reheats leftovers, bakes a cake on Sundays, simple cakes from yeast dough with crumble on top, or cakes with fruit. Maja gets the last dry piece on Thursdays after supper. Her aunt ensures that the child grows, that she is clean and gets plenty to eat. Constant questions don't satisfy you; she still needs to teach Maja that questions are for asking about someone's health, the weather, if a person's hungry, or even whether the table has been set or the meal is ready.

It is chilly in the parlour; Maja draws the red blanket around her shoulders. There's paper and kindling in the stove ready just in case it needs lighting. Her father owes his life to this stove, her aunt once told her. The winter he was born was particularly harsh and the stove was lit regularly. Her aunt had wrapped the frail baby in cloths and placed him in a basket on the tiled seat.

But she said nothing about the cards, and she never spoke about why Maja's father had gone away either, just as she had got used to calling him Papa.

Maja's memory focuses on the moment when she had entered the house for the first time. Her father had gone ahead of her and sat at the shiny wooden table; Maja stayed standing in the doorway and didn't understand what her aunt wanted from her.

Don't just stand in the doorway, she must have said; that's what her aunt always says whenever Maja leans against the doorframe, waiting for her aunt to thrust the tea towel into her hand or point at the kitchen dresser with her chin when it is time for Maja to set the table.

It was dusky in the room; Maja had counted the little windows; *adzin, dva, try*; she could already count to ten but there were only three. Three little windows in thick stone walls, a wood-panelled ceiling. A lamp with a linen shade above the dining table gave out a feeble light. Her aunt turned her back to her and rattled cutlery; something was cooking on the stove. Maja didn't recognize the smell rising from the pot and couldn't even decide whether it was pleasant or not. She stood, rooted in the doorway, looking in turn from her father to her aunt and back again. Her father's face was half in shadow. No one was looking at her, her aunt placed a glass of milk on the table in front of her father, then stirred the saucepan; her father was staring at the tabletop. Well then, he said. And he repeated, well. After a time that seemed endless to Maja, her aunt took a step or two towards her. Maja stood in front of the flower-patterned skirt of her apron; her aunt wiped her wet hands on it and pushed her towards the table. Maja sat down opposite her father, watching as he drank his milk. He had visited her in the children's home; the matron had led Maja to understand that he was her father and this father had taken her for a walk and treated her to ice-cream – strawberry ice-cream. When they returned to the home, Maja stood in the middle of the playroom. Strawberry ice-cream, she shouted, pointing to her mouth and her dress which was flecked with pink spots. A girl had stood in front of her, ran her tongue over Maja's lips, then the screaming began, and a care worker came in looking severe and, without a word, grabbed the girl under the arms and carried her out of the room.

Sometime later the same care worker had packed a few pieces of clothing into a bag with the Matryoshka on top, put Maja's shoes on her and pushed her outside the door to where her father was waiting. She had to go with him because her mother was lying under the ground so her father was going to look after her.

Maja's aunt put a glass of warm milk in front of her, sprinkled a little cocoa powder into it, stirred it noisily and gestured for her to drink. She sat down with them, looked at Maja, then stretched out her arm and patted the child's head.

Whatever will be, will be, she said.

Her father said nothing.

The clock in the parlour strikes three; her aunt will be back in an hour. The stove is cold. The clock chimes echo, and the feeble afternoon sun makes the room seem darker than before. Maja unwraps herself from the rug and listens to see if everything is really quiet in the house, puts her two feet down together on the ground and, although she is alone, she chooses the quiet path, moving on tiptoe, to the larder. Wood creaks somewhere – the wall panelling in the hall perhaps, or the floor. Maja starts, but everything remains quiet; it was only the house. She places her hand on the door handle, hoping her aunt has not locked it. The door opens; it smells of onions and smoked sausage. Maja stands on tiptoe to reach the light switch hanging on a cable from the ceiling. The light flickers, then steadies, lighting up the shelves of the forbidden room, the room only her aunt is permitted to enter. But there's nothing here to attract a child, just tightly sealed jars of jams, packages of sugar and flour, pots of fat, vegetables, bread that is left lying there for three days before her aunt cuts it so that they won't eat too much. Her aunt disappeared in there after she had read her father's last card aloud for Maja:

My Dears, Happy Easter.

Maja searches shelf by shelf, pushing a stepladder from the farthest corner of the room into the middle and feeling along the highest shelf. She feels something with sharp corners – hard, stiff cardboard. Her fingertips claw at it but she is unable to draw it towards her. Then she gets a grip on an edge of its cover, digs her fingers under the edge and, bit by bit, draws the box towards her until she can hold it in both hands. It is light, lighter than she had expected. Maja places the box on the stepladder, lifts the cover and takes out card after card. She can't read her father's writing although the teacher has praised her for learning her letters so quickly, more quickly than the other children, but her father's writing spreads in great bows over the limited space on the postcards. It is like a track in the snow, looped and illegible, pressed into the cold white by fallen twigs or little heaps of snow that have fallen in thick drops from the branches. Maja holds Easter bunnies, Christmas trees and birthday cakes up to the light; she holds the written side at an angle, traces her index finger over it, breathes on it, dampens her finger with spit, wipes the moisture carefully over the card but it doesn't reveal any secret writing – nothing had been written and then erased.

My Dears, Happy Easter, now Maja has to believe her aunt; a stack of punctual wishes lie in an old box without any secret compartment.

Maja puts the box back, touches the onions, sausages and bread, smells her fingers, switches off the light, closes the door and goes up the stairs to her bedroom. She lies on her bed, hiding under the thick feather-quilt, taking care that there are no stray locks of hair left showing; she stretches her legs straight out so that her knees don't create a hill and waits until her breathing slows. She breathes in and out; the air becomes warm and thick, thick like the syrup she is not allowed to drink undiluted. She makes a little airhole on the wall side and closes her eyes. She sees onions and bread, flickering light, sees herself feeling the shelves, feeling everything that she sees. Dust clings to her fingertips and she licks it off. It's like sugar, why has nobody ever told her that dust tastes like sugar. There's more higher up, she stretches, wanting to reach the highest shelf. Her feet leave the ground. It's so easy, you just have to want it hard enough. She sways a little in the air, rises higher and, stretching her arms, grabs tightly onto the shelf. Instead of dust, she sees birthday cakes there, one beside the other. She wants to stick her finger into the cream, but the brightly coloured cream icing feels stiff and dried out; the cakes are made of cardboard with hard sugar hearts stuck on them. Maja breaks one off, a rosy-pink dried out sugar heart. There's a loud crack as she breaks it off, it snaps again, and again like an echo even though she only took a small piece. Suddenly cold air streams in and the cracking sound stops; her aunt's wooden clogs are beside Maja's bed and her hands have pulled the quilt off her with an energetic tug.

Sleeping in the daytime, that's not on, you can't do that here, she says. The cardboard cakes disappear along with the hearts, the sugar, the floating. Not in my house, her aunt says, not loudly but almost softly, so firmly that Maja's eyes fill with tears, and she gets up without a word, shakes the pillow and quilt out, and follows her aunt, who doesn't say another word but uses her chin to point at the kitchen door, the kitchen dresser, the table and, a little later, the bread knife and the saucepan to boil water for tea.

You can't do that, she says then as she sits down at the table, I'm not rearing a layabout. Maja knows that she has no reason to cry. Her aunt doesn't shout or hit her, and Maja imagines the water in her eyes seeping away before it can run down her cheeks. She imagines this very hard so that her aunt will see that she's sensible, a big girl, and she succeeds; she swallows her tears and promises to make herself useful, even on Sunday.

Her aunt puts a piece of cake in front of her, a yeast cake with crumble, a fresh Sunday slice.

It's not easy for you, child, her aunt says then, now eat up.

The teacher has shown them how to fold paper, corner to corner, edge to edge. Maja strokes the fold smooth with her thumbnail and bends the resulting corners upwards; she tugs patiently to reveal tiny paws and a tail. Then she straightens the horns and adds paper animals one by one to her menagerie. Her aunt asks if Fini makes paper animals too and Maja nods. Her aunt is knitting a rug; variously coloured scraps of wool twitch alternately out of her wicker-basket. Though Maja feels the cold stove tiles against her back, she leans against it; it is her place, evening after evening. Tomorrow afternoon, she will go to Fini or to Marek and in the evening, she will read a page and write a few lines and her aunt will let her knitting jerk as she looks across the room every now and then, to check if Maja is focussing on her books.

The deer is ready. Maja bends his legs apart, tweaks his antlers and uses a needle to make a hole in his back so that she can hang him up using a transparent plastic thread. Maja hangs him up in front of the window with the other paper animals. They sway in the draught and Maja watches as the animals dance.

She wants to hang deers on all the windows, and foxes and ravens and doves and a butterfly and pearls of polished glass that break up the light and reflect and throw light patterns onto the whitewashed walls. Her aunt has no objection.

If that's the only thing you do to upset me, she says, and Maja shakes her head answering, no, I won't cause any upset, and she pulls a golden bow out of her schoolbag. This will become the butterfly.

It had been easy to sneak the sheet of paper into her bag; the shining sheets were tempting, just lying there on the teacher's table. Even Fini hadn't noticed anything although she was sitting next to her the whole time and Maja said nothing to her. She wants the golden butterfly just for herself. If all those remaining hours of school with a bad conscience were going to be worth it, the corners had to be perfect as every adjustment would show afterwards. The butterfly was more difficult to fold than the raven and even the deer; it had to work on the first attempt if its golden wings were to dance in the light, and it had to twirl more beautifully than all the other animals.

Her aunt gets up to fetch new wool. There is a basket behind the door, half-full of toy building bricks and there are wool scraps of every colour on top. Once, when Maja had only been with her aunt for a few months and was

24

only four years old, Marek had called around and brought her coloured bricks, a doll and soap bubbles.

So that she has something to play with, he had said, and her aunt had pointed with her chin towards Maja who was sitting on a rag rug in the corner trying to build a house out of bits of wood.

She has something, her aunt had said but remained standing at the stove when Marek bent down to the child and spread his gifts out in front of her.

You say thank you, her aunt had murmured.

That's okay, Marek had said, putting his cap on as he left. One day her aunt had braided Maja's hair into two plaits, dressed her in her nicest dress, polished boots and a warm jacket, and the two of them pushed their way through drifting snow to Marek's house. Her aunt had advised her what she had to say nicely, and things would be okay. She made her understand that Marek was a poor fish and nobody in the village really knew why he was here, but they were decent people and decent people said thanks whenever they got a present.

Maja had been scared about reciting the sentences; the children's laughter remained in her head long after she had asked the teacher what the word piss meant. Fini was the only one who hadn't laughed; she took her by the hand and promised to sit beside her next year and explain everything to her, word of honour.

Now, her hand clamped in her aunt's, Maja whispered out the sentences and when Marek opened the door nothing but a stammer came out, and then tears and then Marek invited the pair of them in and poured tea for her aunt and a glass of raspberry juice for the child, and he looked at Maja in a way that let the sentences flow and her aunt finally let Maja's hand go and Maja drank the juice and looked around the room and couldn't see the fish her aunt had spoken about anywhere.

Come child, help me, her aunt says, and Maja puts the golden paper aside and bends her arms. Her aunt hangs the wool on Maja's stiff outstretched fingers and winds it into a tight ball. Come child, help me, her aunt says when a basket is too heavy for her or when she can't find something. Eat child, her aunt says when she places a plate in front of Maja.

Maja is clean, she is full; she washed the crumbs from the Sunday cake off her fingers immediately after supper. Soon it will be time for bed. Like in the parlour, there's only one lamp hanging in the kitchen; her aunt's face is half in shadow, the growing ball of wool is in the light, Maja's eyes close.

At night she can sleep unpunished in her feathery cave, lying soft and warm. Whenever Maja moves even just a little, the quilt rustles like the fabric of an evening dress;

and sometimes Maja believes she can smell something delicate, a hint of expensive perfume. The smell stays by her bed until she falls asleep and, only when she is dreaming, does the rustle fade away; softly, quietly so as not to waken the child, it wafts across the floorboards.

III
Warm Raspberries

Not today, no, she's not coming today anyway, Marek thinks, turning away from the window. He reaches out his hand for the water glass, hesitates, then picks it up after all and replaces it in the crockery cupboard.

And the cordial bottle, he murmurs, after smoothing the tablecloth, the one embroidered with songbirds, before opening the door to the larder. It is no more than a niche in the wall, just a couple of boards fastened with various screws and protruding dowels. The shelves have bowed under the weight of jars of preserves, tins and bottles, Marek realized too late that the heavier items would be better placed at the ends. He places the cordial bottle on the top shelf and takes down a tin of sauerkraut and some preserved mushrooms. It is getting dark, he can just about discern the shape of the bushes in the garden and, with darkness falling, the cold creeps into the house, or perhaps it was there all the time, and he only feels it now. He will give old Walter money to clear the bushes for once and for all, he wants to be able to see as far as the fence, as far as his fence, its wood which has become as grey as the walls of his house.

Marek lights the stove, spoons fat into a cast iron pan and fries the mushrooms, finely chopped meat, onions and sauerkraut. He cuts a slice of bread from a dark loaf. It's a long time since he's made dough for wrapping around the filling.

Not today either, he tells himself, no, she didn't come today. He stirs the food in the pan, takes it off the stove and places it on the table. He leaves the curtains open; the lamp is reflected on the windowpane, and he can still see a few twigs scratching the window but he doesn't see the moon. He opens the newspaper lying on the window seat. There is a new moon tomorrow and it is going to snow. He had forgotten; he had read that in the morning and forgotten again. It's not that important what kind of moon it is, Marek thinks, still shaking his head at himself and the fact that he had forgotten reading about the new moon and the snow.

He eats straight from the pan, it's tasty, last year was a good year for mushrooms. Bread goes well with it. And tea, he hasn't made the tea yet. He puts his hands on the table to support himself as he gets up, turns the stove on again and runs water into the kettle. It will have to be black tea with sugar, the dried mint Maja brought is hanging like an upside-down bouquet on a nail above the sink. Marek waits until the water boils, then wets the tea. He will get up early tomorrow, shave and then go to the doctor, his leg has got worse. Perhaps it's the snow, Marek thinks. The doctor will tell him that the medicine will make him tired and is bad for his liver. This liver is old enough, Marek will answer, and I am tired ever since I can think. It is just the pain, no, he can't bear the pain anymore. The doctor owes him that much – a pain-free leg.

Marek wears woollen socks and slippers; he has bound the left slipper together with sticky tape because the sole was coming off. His slippers are made of grey felt with different coloured stains gathered from cooking, cleaning his teeth, or when he has poured the raspberry juice Fini's mother cooks into a thick syrup year after year in late summer and always gives him a few bottles to dilute with warm water or with soda water for a treat, reminding him of his childhood. Marek's childhood smells of warm raspberries with sweet cream; it smells of damp moss, of river water, of the two cows that gave them all such joy and his parents' sweat. Now in winter, when the smell of cold wind, snow, and smoke hangs stubbornly between the houses, the images return. Marek sits on the wooden bench, looks at the mullion and transom of the window, at the ice-flowers and he tries to forget what followed the raspberries and river water and the cows. A quiet happiness helps in forgetting, a quiet happiness reaches out a hand to him; he just needs to grasp it. He takes Maja by the hand when she stands at his door with a rosy face, breathless from running.

Come on in, Marek says and Maja goes right across the room to the chest covered with a little woven rug, sits on it, smiles and looks at him expectantly, watching him without a word, the way he moves around the kitchen, getting a glass from the shelf, the way he eventually pours the raspberry syrup and fetches a bottle of sparkling water from the pantry – *Sprudelwasser*, what sort of a word is that, Marek had said the first time and Maja laughed. He makes the juice deep red for Maja.

This is so you'll remember it later on, he says to Maja, so that you will say, Marek always made deep-red raspberry juice for me.

His leg's giving him no peace today, he will wash up tomorrow. He clasps the warm teacup with both hands. His skin is wrinkled and red, his nails thick and yellowish; he will always have those callouses from working with wood. When the images come, those scraps of memories, he hears screams, smells the sweat, feels the bodies of the adults who could not tell him where they were being brought. His wet trousers, the apple he was still holding in his hands, the trousers his mother had sewn out of curtain material. Evening after evening, she had sat, red-eyed, on the stove bench, pushing the sewing needle through the thick fabric, stitch by stitch.

His mother's eyes. Her look as the soldiers tore her away from him and pushed her towards the other women. Her mouth, opening in a scream, her last words to him, which he could not hear because the shouts, cries and whimpers drowned them out. He was shoved towards the boys and stronger people, a soldier kicked him in the hollow of the knee when he wouldn't turn around.

The cold crossbar of the wagon door at his back. The man who was sitting crouched on the ground biting his fingers until they bled. The swaying of the wagon. His eye on the chink in the door. The whispering: what can you see? Where are we? Tell us, what do you see?

The names of the stations soon meant nothing to him; the train stopped for hours by a bridge over a river: *Dunaj*, someone whispered, *Dunaj, Dunaj*, it was like a magic spell that he was sending back into the dark water as far as the Black Sea.

Dark pine woods at last, standing in the distance like walls. Silence when the train stopped, getting out in the middle of an open field. The raw wooden shed which they had to endure for weeks before they were brought to the barracks. The woman who threw them something to eat over the fence, her reassuring words, *Glück,* the first German word he learned: *ihrhabt Glück gehapt –* youwerein luck. He ensnared this sentence with his lips, shaping it for himself, without understanding what it meant.

Ten minutes away from the barracks was a farm, they had to repair a broken fence there. The snow had caused it to collapse and soon it would be time to let the cattle out on the meadows. Like the others, Marek was sinking to his shins in the mud and had to dig his clogs out carefully with his fingers when he needed to take a step forward or sideways. One day the farmer's wife was suddenly standing in front of him, reaching a bundle towards him.

There, for you. She seemed to be in a hurry, looking around to check that she was not being watched.

Two shirts and a pair of trousers; be careful, there's something else in it, she said.

She stroked his hair that was stiff with dirt.

You're still a child, a child, fallen out of the nest too early.

Then she turned around and hurried back to the farmhouse.

Marek hadn't even been able to say thank you, he didn't know what had happened to him. It seemed nobody had noticed. Everyone was preoccupied, and the overseers were out of sight. Marek smelled the bundle, it smelled of bread, then he hid it behind a tree and went on with his work.

A couple of school children went by on the trailer of a tractor. *Polacks, Polacks*, they shouted and spat down on them. One boy stood up, pulled his trousers down and waggled his bottom at them. That burned more than the sewn-on 'P' that Marek had to wear on his chest; the jeering of the children burrowed into him.

They met nobody in the woods, remaining alone with the cracking of the wood, the striking of the axes. With the low-lying clouds and incessant rain, the trees offered almost no shelter. The barracks were a half-day's march away. Four of them cowered together under an old tarpaulin and tried to sleep. Marek clutched his leg; the bones would grow together badly but the splints held. Some of the men had lost their lives in the woods. He was in luck – it was only his leg.

The older men had built themselves a shelter out of planks; they whispered in the damp darkness. Marek had noticed an unrest among the men in the last few days, perceptible in whispers; the overseers' eyes appeared more haunted than usual. What if everything was coming to an end? What then? Fear crept over him. If there was nobody waiting for him, if strangers were living on their farm, was the farm even still there? Maybe strange children were sleeping in his bed, playing with daddy-longlegs before going to sleep, as he had done. Waiting for summer, to eat warm raspberries, to help his father and his brothers in the fields, stealing away from them to hunt lizards and stuff their tails as trophies into his trouser pockets.

Not a word was uttered while the tree trunks were being loaded up, not even a whisper; water ran under their clothes, along their cold skin and into their wooden shoes. There was no end to the rain in sight as they made their way back on foot. Marek took his wooden shoes in his hands and walked barefoot through the cold sludge; he could no longer feel anything anyhow.

In the barracks the men threw a few bits of wood into the stove and some of them massaged their feet. One man tore a strip of fabric from his shirt to bandage a bloody wound on his arm.

Then the door opened and one of the overseers roared Marek's name, thrust the sodden envelope at him without another word, then turned on his heel and left, leaving the door open. Marek staggered backwards, holding the letter in both hands, as Adam grabbed his arm and pressed him down on his bunk beside him.

Sit here beside me, he said, watching as Marek tore one corner of the envelope, stuck his finger into the hole, moving it over and back like a letter opener. Then Adam helped Marek to read the news, pointing with his finger at words and letters.

Marek remembered the damp atmosphere of the barracks, the rain beating unceasingly on the metal roof, the earthy spring air released from the ground, the smell of sweat and rotten wood rising between the bunks and the stolen potatoes that someone had laid on the single stove.

Adam didn't read aloud to Marek; the paper had to be the messenger, not him. The writing was smudged, but they both knew what it would say even as they unfolded the letter. Marek did not let the paper fall and he didn't cry. He sat there, stiff, unable to feel anything. The men coughed; someone swore. Adam looked at Marek, whispered, now your mother too. A spider vanished into a crack in the ground, came out again after a short time, and ran across the room. Marek sat upright for several minutes. He wished that his mother had fallen in the quarry or that she had been shot from behind because she hadn't lowered her gaze from the overseer, that she simply didn't open her eyes some morning. Her warm, dark blue eyes. Marek pressed his fist to his teeth, then the shivering started; shivering replaced the crying, screaming, whimpering, as if his body was taking over, doing what his spirit could not afford to do.

The men had not cried for themselves for a long time, not from pain, when something hurt their own bodies, when the guards' hands beat down on their heads and burst their eardrums, when rifle butts struck their disobedient legs or backs as they bent down to steal potatoes. Adam watched Marek sideways. But children must cry, he whispered, taking the letter from Marek's hand, come here.

And he let him sleep on his pallet, this fourteen-year-old; he held him in his arms until dawn and waited in vain for tears.

A year later, a new spring rain had softened the earth and a forester was looking for helpers a few kilometres away, and because Marek had learned nothing apart from felling trees and sawing off branches, loading trunks and splitting fire timber, he went after the forester and into another forest where he fell in love with Anna, but she did not want him and he had gazed after her fluffy hair and red cheeks, her soft round belly. Then he was left alone in this little hut, which he had bought, bit by bit, and which he now owned. In winter it was covered with snow and the rain hammered on the roof in summer. The sound penetrating the house was muffled, however, and it had lost its power to threaten him. And years later, he stood at his window glancing out into the garden, over the fence separating his house from the road, not the road from his house and, surprised at the salty taste on his lips, in disbelief he felt his cheeks, which were wet: wet wrinkled skin, and he had just looked out at the rich, green shrubbery.

Marek massages his leg; his cup is empty. It is a pity that Maja did not come. But tomorrow, perhaps. She will swing her legs and wait for raspberry juice and a story. And when you're grown up, Maja, you must remember that Marek waited in his own house for you, he watched out to the fence and beyond; he always made you deep-red raspberry juice. Maja, remember that; you must remember.

IV
One Hundred Brushstrokes

Her white teeth, Maja thinks, white teeth when she laughs.

You need to clean them with salt, Fini said, every second day, then your teeth will be just as white. Maja tried spreading salt on her toothbrush and then rubbing her teeth, but it made her retch. She spat out the salt and rinsed and rinsed until the salt taste was gone. She didn't tell Fini about it, she said, I can't do anything about it, so I will just have to live with these teeth.

Take your clothes off, Fini cried, we'll see what your best points are. And she shoved Maja in front of the mirror and watched as she took off her trousers, blouse, underwear and turned around uncertainly in front of Fini.

Lift your arms, Fini said, and Maja turned around again and then put her underwear, blouse and trousers back on.

And what do you think? she asked then. Fini took her chin between her thumb and index finger and looked up at the ceiling as if she were making up her mind.

Tell me, said Maja.

Your hair, your hair, and your legs. With legs like yours you will find a man.

Fini lies with her face to the wall. Her breath is steady: she has covered only her legs; her head sinks into the pillow. The window is wide open, the sun shining partway into the room, as far as the rug and no further. Maja holds Fini's cut-off hair in her hand, a thick hank, Fini didn't want a plait.

Throw it away, she had said, I don't want to see it anymore.

She was in her nightgown, sitting on the chair in front of her desk. She had balanced the hand mirror carelessly against the crooked stack of books and copies in front of her.

She sought Maja's eyes in the mirror: Now. Her voice sounded strong; she was sure of herself.

And so, Maja had taken the scissors and tried to cut in a line. Hair fell to the ground, lock by lock. Fini's neck was laid bare, with its fine fluffy hair. When it was all level with Fini's chin, she took the scissors from Maja's hand and ran her fingers through her hair like a comb. Clumping individual locks between her fingers, she stretched them upwards, cutting quickly, forwards, backwards, above her ears. The sound of the scissors was like a grazing animal. A dark heap lay on the ground and dark strands fell criss-cross over Fini's shoulders. Maja stood behind Fini, looking over her head into the mirror, at the concentration on Fini's face, her compressed lips, her cheeks, the mascara smeared under her eyes.

That's enough, said Maja after a while, when Fini continued cutting, going ever more quickly over her head, cutting without even looking properly. That's enough, Maja cried, ripping the scissors out of her hand. She stood there aghast, looking at Fini, who was sitting stiff in front of the mirror, stroking her short hair, over and over. Then Fini took off her nightgown. Still seated, she drew it carefully over her hips and Maja helped her pull it over her head. Maja shook it out; the hair didn't want to leave the fabric. Fini stroked her hands over her face, her neck, her shoulders and wiped the hair off her skin, grinning at Maja as she stood up. Well? Good? she asked, pale now, her legs were giving way; she shouldn't have stood up so quickly. Maja reached out an arm, supported her and Fini got into bed, just as she was.

Don't you want to put some clothes on? Maja asked.

Why? answered Fini. Perhaps the air will draw out the fever; open the window.

At least cover yourself, said Maja, please. And Fini turned over on her side, pulling the covers up to her thighs. Then she murmured something else, thank you perhaps, but Maja was not sure what; she fell asleep like a small child, from one moment to the next.

From the ground floor Maja hears a hum, the bread machine perhaps. She kneels on the tiled floor, sweeping a clump of hair together with her hand and stuffing it into a plastic bag. Pretty Fini, just lying there. She would have liked to say, soon you will be well again, we can go outdoors to the stream and lie down in the sun, we won't have missed anything; warm days are on the way. She would have liked to roam through the woods with her, to stand by and watch her climbing awkwardly up the cliffs in her red sandals, which made even walking hard. She would have liked to feel the warm rock under her, and hear Fini's breath beside her, to take her hand and whisper in her ear, listen, I want to tell you something. She didn't want to look at Fini while she was talking; she wanted to look up at the sky and speak as if she were talking to herself. About Marek and the rag rug, the narrow corner bench in front of the window with the branches from the garden scratching the panes, the glass animals he had given her for her birthday, about things she would have preferred to leave alone. Then just don't go there anymore, Fini would have said, nobody is forcing you.

Maja leaves the bag beside the door and listens to Fini's breathing again, then goes quietly over to her bed, covers her properly and closes the window.

They've put on make-up, for no particular reason, thick black eyeliner and lipstick. Maja had put mascara on Fini's eyelashes and rouge on her cheeks. Her skin was warm under Maja's fingers, her warm pale skin. They take it in turns to look in the hand mirror and Fini says, at least now the doctor has something to look at. And then she tells Maja that her mother sneaks through the house at night, murmuring to herself; she is worried and has nobody to talk to because Erich is away.

But she has you, Maja says, trying to imagine Fini's mother in a nightdress, walking from room to room in her bare feet, maybe smelling freshly baked bread and carefully covering it with an embroidered tea towel again. Perhaps she wrings her hands and looks out at the dark garden. In Maja's imagination Fini's mother has her aunt's face and her hands. Her aunt slips through the house, surreptitiously smelling the bread, breaking off a little piece and sticking it hurriedly into her mouth. It is so fresh it melts on her tongue. She swallows, talking quietly to herself, things that remain unspoken, things not for Maja's ears, pulls her knitted jacket tighter and stops in front of the pictures in the living room, looking at the family: Fini, Erich, her mother and the way they laugh and hug one another.

Maja doesn't want to create a picture that matches Fini's mother.

Fini's mother always knocks before she enters the room. Her steps warn that she is coming, the clack of wooden clogs on the hall below, the rhythmic change on the stairs. Her mother strokes Fini's hair and speaks to her softly because Maja is there and shouldn't hear anything. There's a film of glass around the two of them, separating Maja from Fini. What must it feel like to have a mother's mouth so close to your ear, her breath ruffling some of your hair, the bits around your ear and neck and arms.

Fini rolls her eyes when their glances meet and presses her mother's hand before she pushes her away from her shoulder.

The copied pages are lying in a heap on Fini's desk.

I can't study, she says, the letters just dance in front of my eyes, look, just like that. And she climbs out of bed and sweeps pages, copies and books off the desk with a hefty shove, takes Maja's hand and swirls round the room with her.

I can't study, I can't read, she shouts, what a pity, and she laughs as she speaks. Maja tries to escape her grip, but Fini quickly grabs her around the waist and won't let her go until Maja shouts, stop that, go and lie down again.

Fini sits on the bed tapping the mattress with her hand.

Come here, sit beside me, she says. Or no, can you put on some music first? Maja presses the button on the tape recorder. Fini pretends to play the guitar, singing along in her hoarse voice.

What's going to become of us? she asks and laughs.

What's wrong with you? Maja asks, calm down, you have a fever, lie down. She grabs Fini by the shoulder, pushing her onto the mattress, feeling the resistance slowly ebbing from Fini's body. Fini turns her face to the wall.

What did the doctor say? Maja asks, does he even know what's wrong with you?

Fini doesn't move, it's only a while later that she moves her head slowly over and back, a lying down shake of the head.

Have a little sleep, says Maja, I'll fetch your mother. Maja stays sitting on the bed for another minute, but Fini doesn't say anything else and keeps her eyes shut. Maja gets up and goes down the wooden stairs to tell Fini's mother. They come back together and Fini's mother feels her forehead, asks Maja if she would like to take another piece of cake home with her and thanks her for coming. Thank you, she says, it's very important for Fini.

Wait and see, the doctor had said. After another couple of weeks, Fini's mother stands outside the school and tells Maja she doesn't need to take any more notes for her daughter – she won't be able to make up the whole year.

Nevertheless, Maja brings her homework every second day, as she has been doing for weeks now. She sees how the pile on the desk has got even bigger, how her friend is even thinner, her hair is falling out and her skin looks transparent. None of her clothes will fit her when she gets better again.

When I get better, Fini had said, I want to look brand new, new hairstyle, new clothes. I'll give you my clothes, trousers, blouses – pick what you want. I'll give you everything.

Maja had been ashamed last autumn when Fini had emerged from the toilet in ripped shorts and fishnet tights. Fini had put on make-up, pulled her hair into a bun and stashed the clothes she had worn leaving home in her handbag. She looked older, about twenty, standing beside the door until Maja came to her.

We can't go like that, Maja had said.

Why not, nobody's going to know us, Fini answered. She pressed her lips together to even out the lipstick and pulled Maja towards her, planting a kiss on her cheek. Pretty, she said. Maja wiped off the red print; she wanted to have a nice day, eat ice-cream, look at the displays in the shop windows and take a walk in the park. And now this, everyone would turn around to look at Fini and then at her.

Don't be such a spoilsport, said Fini, come on! She took Maja by the hand, pulling her outside. On the right side of the town square was a group of people making noise, holding banners aloft and banging drums. Some of them were sitting in a circle on the ground. As Maja tried to make out the words on the banners, she was jostled by a young woman who pressed a flyer into her hand, talking at her and pointing at the trees in the middle of the square. Fini let Maja's hand go and stood in front of a bookshop window, feigning interest. She ran her hands covertly over her hips and looked over her shoulder at Maja and the young woman.

Which way? Fini asked as Maja came towards her, her fingernails tapped on the shop window following the drum rhythm.

At lunchtime they went into a Chinese restaurant – this was their birthday present to each other. They stood uncertainly in front of the buffet before deciding to take a bit of everything, balancing their heaped plates as they moved towards their table. Some brown sauce splashed over the edge of Maja's plate onto her shoe. Maja placed her plate on the white tablecloth, bent down and wiped her shoe with a corner of the cotton serviette. Sauce and street dirt smudging the white fabric, Maja folded it up so that the stain didn't show and stuck it under her plate.

No, you're supposed to do it this way, said Fini, spreading her serviette on her lap and, removing the chopsticks from their wrappings, she tried to pick up the fried noodles.

A couple were sitting at the next table; the woman silently spooned up soup while her husband turned his head to look at Fini.

Good, said Fini, without noticing his glance, what do you think?

Maja nodded, looking away quickly as the man noticed her watching him. This was going to be her day, her belated birthday celebration, without having to worry about what she had to do for her aunt and no heavy shopping bag pulling on her arm. They would get the last bus and she would take her new neck scarf and long necklace of wooden balls out of their shining cellophane papers and hold them up to the weak light, put the scarf and then the necklet around her neck, then change them again. She would imagine what it would be like not to go back to the village, to get into another bed, walk along other streets, perhaps in a big city.

They missed the bus because they hadn't checked the departure time properly. They sat beside each other on the edge of the pavement at the empty bus stop, surprised at being the only passengers, then started getting worried when the bus didn't arrive. After ten minutes Fini stood up, walked over to the notice board and swore.

What's up? Maja asked, although she knew exactly, there wouldn't be another bus; tell us, what's up?

The shutters were already down on all the shops; a taxi full of well-dressed people drove by them.

How much money have you left? Fini asked and Maja pulled out her wallet and counted; there was nothing like enough for a taxi.

What about you? Fini had only a couple of coins, just enough for the bus fare.

We'll walk, said Maja, let's walk, there's no point in staying here.

Fini opened her bag, took out her crumpled skirt and pulled it on over her shorts, right there on the street, but there was nobody to see her. She fumbled around under the fabric to take off the shorts, but she kept the fishnet tights on. Stray strands were falling out of her hair-knot and her lipstick was entirely gone.

It will take us at least three hours in these shoes, she told Maja.

Have we any choice, said Maja.

The country road was dark. They walked in single file along the ditch, seeing lights, some cars and a motorbike approaching them.

What if someone wants to give us a lift? Fini asked.

I don't know, said Maja. Her feet hurt even though she was wearing flat shoes. Fini didn't complain but she must have had blisters, it would be impossible not to.

Okay, if we know them, said Maja.

Fini said nothing. There was just the sound of her heels on the road. Then there was the sound of a car from behind, the cat's eyes on the centre line lit up. Fini turned around and stretched her arm out, her thumb in the air.

A small truck drove by, turned on the hazards and stopped, an unknown registration.

No, hissed Maja as the passenger door was already opening. Fini sprang forward. Maja watched as she spoke to the driver, then turned back to Maja, waving her forwards and Maja thought she could see her smiling.

Her aunt didn't complain when Maja got home. She sent her for a bath. Maja washed the day from her skin, the city air and the cigarette smell from the truck. As she lay in bed she thought of the driver and about Fini who had never stopped talking, the soft music on the truck radio, the cones of light from the headlights on the road, that it could just as easily have been a woman driving, or a couple. But it had been a young man. And he hadn't done anything to them. And he had dropped Fini off first, then left her at her door and waited until the door opened.

Do you know about Erich? Fini asks her.

Maja nods. Of course, she knows but she doesn't like thinking about the shed in the woods where Fini's brother disappeared with a girl from the town. What are they up to? Fini said, let's go, I need to find out. And she had grabbed Maja by the hand and dragged her to the shed; the door was slightly ajar and Maja had a clear view of Erich's sweaty face. She held her breath, looked, looked away. Then, taking a couple of careful steps backwards, she turned around and ran, into the woods, scratching her arms and legs on twigs until eventually she reached the narrow path to the stream, and ran onwards, past the forester's four-by-four down on the bank, then through the meadow behind her aunt's house. Maja threw herself down on the grass, one cheek pressed into the earth, prickly stalks around her, just-mown meadow. She inhaled its scent and the smell of the earth and looked at the blades of grass, an ant, two, a butterfly, a beetle, insects as they crept undisturbed through the grass. Erich and the girl from the town.

On Monday at school, Fini wanted to know why Maja had run away. It's only natural, she said, everyone does it at some stage. And Erich had looked up as Fini ran away but he hadn't actually seen her, and he just kept going. And anyway, it was all over between the two of them, she said, her brother had bad luck with girls. Yesterday, he had sat at the table looking serious and said that he was going to work weekends as well and wouldn't be visiting home for a while.

The day when Maja and Fini had stood by the closed front door. It had rained and they sat on the steps under the little porch roof, crouching close together because the wind was driving the rain in under the roof. Maja's aunt was in town and the two girls had been supposed to eat in Fini's house, then read and do their maths homework and study. As a reward, they could stroke the rabbits and give the hens a sneaky chase.

Fini's mother came home after hours, walking upright as if someone had tied a stick to her back, her expression fixed and staring ahead. The girls jumped up; Fini ran a few strides towards her mother, stopping suddenly as if an invisible hand were holding her back from reaching out to hug her.

They found your father, her mother said, and still moving, she pulled the house key out of her handbag and opened the door, going ahead of them, past the kitchen and straight upstairs. She turned around on the top step.

I'll make you something to eat later, go and play.

The girls heard her footsteps upstairs, walking back and forth in her room. Fini went into the parlour and sat on the floor near the stove, laying her chin on her knees, her arms around her head. She sat there, completely still and Maja remained in the middle of the room, baffled; she didn't understand what had happened. Fini didn't have a father.

Fini sits on the bed and laughs. She has red specks on her neck, but she is sitting there laughing because Maja has read a sentence out to her. Maja has pulled a piece of paper out of her trouser pocket. Listen, she said, I thought of a sentence; I've written it down, listen up. And she read it out and Fini laughs.

Maja folds the paper up tiny and puts it away again.

Don't be insulted, says Fini.

I'm not, Maja says.

She had told Marek that Fini was ill, which was true; she was bringing her stuff from school and showing her what was to be done. He asked about Erich, if Maja knew how he was doing. Why Erich? Maja had asked, I don't know. I visit Fini, not him.

One of Fini's dresses tucks around Maja's body as Fini brushes her hair for her.

One hundred brushstrokes will spread the grease through your hair so that it shines, said Fini.

That's enough, says Maja, taking the brush from Fini, tying her hair up into a pony-tail and turning in front of the big mirror. The blue fabric swings around her legs. The dress had looked shorter on Fini; her knees hadn't been covered the day they had gone to the theatre with the class, she could remember that clearly. Fini had pulled up the skirt in the bus to show Maja the black lace underskirt beneath. Maja had admired the fine openwork and let it glide over her hand. As the boys began to change seats, Fini drew the dress up over her thighs, crossed her legs, plucking at the blue fabric until just enough of the black lace was showing for it to look like a coincidence. The seat swapping came to a speedy end as the teacher's warning pierced the rows, but Fini stayed sitting like that until they arrived at the theatre.

Maja pulled the white blouse from the band of her trousers and opened the top button. She was the only person wearing a white blouse and black trousers. White blouse and black trousers: that's what they will all wear, her aunt had thought, young things like that wouldn't go to the theatre in anything else.

Short floral skirts, little chiffon dresses that ended well above the knee. Two girls had even come in jeans, jeans and high heels.

Fini had hung back a few steps in the stairway and Maja was unsure if this was deliberate, if she had decided to try and get sitting between two boys. Before the lights went down, she shrugged an apology, made a signal with her hand that Maja didn't understand and crossed her legs. The girl next to Maja leaned forward, whispered confidentially to the girl in the row in front, giggling started, spreading through the rows of seats and Maja was glad when the performance began.

Fini got dressed – she was wearing trousers, a sweater, and thick socks. She came into the room where Maja was waiting. She was freshly washed and leaning on her mother's arm, pale but laughing.

Bubbles, right up to my chin, she called, do you know how it feels to have a bath after such a long time?

She pressed the nightdress back into her mother's hand. No, she said, today I'm going to get dressed properly. And then she pushed her mother out of the room and asked Maja to dry her hair, to pluck her eyebrows and to help her with the eyeliner.

Everything will be fine she says, pushing a chair towards the open window. She clutches the backrest with both hands, places one foot on the seat and almost loses her balance.

Watch out, Maja cries, reaching out a hand to her.

Help me, says Fini, pointing to the windowsill.

She's so light, Maja thinks as Fini stumbles and sits down beside her, and she's still so pale.

Maja takes her friend's hand as if they were going to shake hands and holds it tight. The early summer sun shines into the girls' faces, they hear the tractors in the fields, the postbus on the turning place below switching off its engine.

Look, Erich's coming, says Fini, Mother didn't say anything. She can't do the heavy work anymore. She phones Erich, it's a long journey, she always says, but he is coming and will stay for the weekend and help her with the flagstones, the garden fence and the roof of the henhouse.

Erich sees the girls and waves up at them.

Just be careful, he calls and then he hugs his mother who leaves the spade standing in the ground and wipes her black fingers on her apron. Erich's broad back, his big hands and the strength that he doesn't need any more.

My son has a good job, Fini's mother tells everyone proudly, he doesn't have to get dirty anymore. He decides for himself when he will close his shop and when he will go home. And she thinks to herself that it was fine to bring up her two children on her own and to put up with all the stories spreading around about their fathers, even though not all of them were true.

My son, she says, now. And people congratulate the mother on Erich, though they whisper among themselves as soon as they turn around, this layabout who used to scare the whole village with his devil's music; he can't have got there by fair means. And as for the daughter, they whisper, nothing good will become of her, just look at her. They whisper but Maja hears it all, everyone does.

These warm days are going to last, we can still go to the stream this year, Fini says.

Yes, says Maja, I think so too.

It is so quiet that not even Fini's breathing can be heard. Maja closes the last button; she has picked out the green dress. She took dress after dress out of Fini's wardrobe, felt the fabric, held them up to the light and against her own body. The green silk feels cool against Maja's skin. It smells of Fini's soap and there's a hint of perfume. Fini is allowed to wear her mother's perfume on feast days, and it has clung to the fabric.

Fini's green dress – her Christmas, Easter and birthday dress. She has never worn it outside. Maja only recognizes it from the photos hanging downstairs in the parlour.

Maja turns in front of the mirror, it suits her. She loosens her plait, looks at herself in half profile and stands on tiptoe. It would be perfect with red high-heeled shoes.

Maja would love to ask why Fini doesn't wear it outside. Instead, she closes the wardrobe doors and stands at the window.

Fini's mother has divided the vegetable patch into sections. She has already sown a row of potatoes. She takes a tuber out of her apron, splits it with the rusty garden knife and lays both halves into the dark furrow. She piles earth over it, patting it firm. Fini is so like her, Maja thinks, with her narrow shoulders and slender hips. The way she holds her head as she climbs carefully over the furrows to the little heap of potatoes beside the bed and lays another handful of tubers into the apron she is holding up. She's like Fini when she walks through the rows to the blackboard in school, or to the washbasin to wash ink off her fingers.

Her mother wipes her fingers on her apron, reaches for a strand of hair and tucks it behind the scarf she has knotted at the back of her neck. She looks down towards the road before she climbs back to the vegetable bed.

Maja sees Marek turning the corner and wonders whether she should sit on Fini's bed but then she stays standing at the window, placing her right hand on the windowsill, ready to wave at him. But Marek doesn't look up, just calls a few words over to Fini's mother and she comes over to the fence, looking around while they chat. Her hands are on the garden fence and his beside them. Marek keeps his eyes on her, listening to her, then raises his hand, turns around and says something as he goes. Fini's mother looks after him for a moment, then goes back to her pile of potatoes, letting the seed potatoes fall from her apron onto the pile, calls Erich and goes behind the house. Perhaps he is looking in the shed for suitable planks for the henhouse or perhaps he is sitting beside the piles of firewood having a smoke.

Erich had raised an eyebrow and winked at her as she and Fini went past him. Fini had planted her feet, step by step in the grass, her friend's arm always within reach. Erich, in his blue work trousers, had smoked, thrown the butt into the hedge and given a testing shake to the ladder leaning against the house wall. Maja calculated. What's seven years anyway, she wondered to herself. Fini nodded briefly at her brother without interrupting her story; she was talking about the teacher who apparently, no definitely, she knew someone who could testify they had seen him in the city with another man, just as they were going into a certain pub. Can you imagine that, Fini asked, and he's a teacher. Maja didn't want to think about the teacher.

It is quiet in the garden; Maja closes her eyes and thinks of Erich, imagining him knocking on her aunt's door just as she is about to go to bed. She imagines Erich talking to her aunt, her aunt saying, alright, but just for a minute; her aunt calls her. She runs quickly down the stairs, bangs the door behind her and pulls Erich between the hazel bushes that can't be seen from the house.

Maja turns away from the window, takes a couple of hair clips from the table and stands in front of the mirror again. She raises her arms, draws her hair together at her neck, lets it fall, draws a straight parting and ties her hair in a knot fastening it tight. She watches her reflection, draws her shoulders down and raises her chin.

Then she hears footsteps on the stairs, she looks towards the door and sees Fini's mother facing her.

She has taken off her garden apron, the headscarf too; her cheeks are red from the sun. She stands a minute on the threshold, looking from Maja to Fini's bed and back, running both her hands over her skirt. Her eyes stay fixed on the bag full of hair, but she says nothing, goes to her daughter and touches her shoulder.

Wake up, she says, it's evening. Maja has to go home.

V
Sour Milk

The milk has gone sour even though it had been in the fridge the whole time. Maja pours the coffee away and white clumps remain lying at the bottom of the sink. She turns on the tap, fills the coffee cup and runs water into the sink until all the clumps are gone.

Tea then, she says to Erich, turning around to find his chair empty. He has left the kitchen without a word. He sneaked out – he's always sneaking, gone suddenly or he turns up beside Maja. At first it startles her, to Erich's amusement. I live here, he said laughing, who else could it be. Yes, who else could it be, Maja thought, but she doesn't like it when he suddenly stands beside or behind her, breathing down her neck or waiting in the doorway until she notices his gaze and his presence.

The milk is sour, Maja calls, I'll make tea.

She puts on the water, goes into the living room, into the bedroom, then out onto the balcony where Erich is standing smoking.

Why don't you say anything? she asks.

I didn't hear you, he says.

The milk is sour, I'm making tea, she says and Erich nods.

Tea then.

Maja reaches for the cigarette packet, then leaves it down. The thermometer reads 25 degrees although it's not even nine o'clock. A sharp shadow divides the floor of the balcony. Maja places her bare foot in the sun, then takes a step backwards onto the still-cool tiles and leans against the concrete wall. Drops of water fall from above, dropping past Maja's balcony flowers.

The neighbour is watering the flowers, says Maja.

Yes, says Erich.

I must water them too, Maja says, pulling off a couple of leaves and collecting them in her left hand. The street is deserted – the dog walkers have already gone back home. The children are playing in backyards or are on their way to the swimming pool, not even a car going past. Maja throws the dried-out flower petals in the ashtray and goes to the other side of the balcony to the pots of herbs, running her hand over the lemon thyme, she smells her hand, rubs lavender between her fingertips and reaches her fingertips towards Erich.

We shouldn't smoke so much she says.

Mmh, says Erich.

He stubs out his cigarette, draws a new one from the pack before offering the packet to Maja. She shakes her head, looking past him. Blue sky, not a cloud to be seen, a day to go to the mountain lake, she thinks, to sink her feet into ice-cold water, to behave as they did that summer that seemed to go on forever. Day after day the blue sky had stretched over the houses and every weekend they had sat into the car, a rug, apples and two bottles of water on the back seat; they had sunned themselves and thrown stones in the water, shaken their heads over the people who still went for a run in the heat, instead of lying on the bank talking and eating apples.

Maja strokes Erich on the arm. He has already laid out the newspapers behind him, pushed the folding chairs into the shade and put the two basil plants from the flower rack on the ground to make space for an ashtray and beer. He looks so content standing there in his striped cotton shorts and the skeleton t-shirt he only wears in bed these days. How he used to infuriate the whole village on those Sundays when he used to go home at eight in the morning, passing the church. The old women would hold their handkerchiefs over their noses and mouths when they saw him coming, as if that could prevent the devil in him getting into their bodies when they breathed in. And yet Erich was polite, he avoided the ladies, didn't stagger but walked purposefully with long steps, as if he had just got up. He would greet the people he met, Sunday after Sunday, although nobody returned the greeting. Maja's aunt didn't go to church very often, but she had often spoken about Erich, especially that somebody needed to straighten that lad out, for once and for all. And that his mother was overburdened with children who did just as they liked. Secretly, Maja had admired Erich and once or twice she had gone with her aunt, just to catch sight of him. The church won't collapse if you visit it once in a while, her aunt had said, and it wouldn't do any harm to join in a few prayers, you might just need them at some stage.

Music from the radio can be heard through the open window. Maja crumbles soil between her fingers. She is going to cut the thyme and use it to make tea in the winter, wrapping her hands around the cup, feeling its warmth and thinking back to the warmth of summer, how it felt standing barefoot on the balcony watching the big drops of water missing her flowers and landing on the dark tarmac below.

I'm going back into the kitchen, says Maja, will you come in?

Yes, says Erich, right away.

The bottles are still standing in the hall; she must ask Erich again to drop them off at the off-licence. Maja picks up a cork, glances briefly in the mirror, hears the water boiling, throws the cork in the bin and takes the teapot off the shelf. Fini had given her the pot.

Even if this isn't a wedding, it's something that belongs to the two of you, she had said, taking Erich's and Maja's hands as they lay beside each other, palms upwards on the table. Close your eyes, she had said, and the next moment Maja had felt the cool porcelain and Fini had hugged her first, then Erich. So that you will stay together, Fini had said, I want to see you both at my wedding. Erich answered that she needed to find a man first. Fini punched his shoulder and then asked Maja to visit her soon. You come to us, Maja had said, you can stay with us, and we will go out together.

This was the beginning, Erich's stories about the city, about his little shop, about his friend Bert, who she could work with. Erich's voice, when he was talking to his mother, his broad back, bent over as he helped in the garden, his teeth bumping against Maja's lips when they kissed, his regular breath, which drove away the heavy stillness of the nights.

Maja's phone is lying on the kitchen table. She picks it up and presses a button. No messages. She cuts a slice of bread, butters it and takes a bite. Some honey, she thinks and dipping her spoon into the honey jar, she lets a golden line fall on the butter, licks the spoon and spreads the honey with the butter knife. Looks at her phone again, really no message. Should she ring Bert? They could go to the lake together; if they agreed a time, it would make it easier to persuade Erich.

Why do you always want to go away, he asks her every time, everything is lovely here.

Maja hears a rattling in the hall. Erich is searching through the chest of drawers.

Have you seen my camera, he asks, and Maja shakes her head.

What do you want to photograph? she asks.

Nothing, I just wanted to look for a picture.

I'll call Bert, says Maja, perhaps we can go to the lake.

Yes, you go, I'll stay here, says Erich, opening the kitchen drawer where they keep the extension cable, chargers, and rubber bands.

What if he doesn't have time? Maja asks.

It's too hot, I'm staying here, says Erich kissing Maja on the mouth and taking a bite of her bread.

Good, he says and disappears again, calling something from the bedroom that Maja doesn't understand. He's probably found the camera, but she doesn't ask, she doesn't care.

She finishes her bread and licks the honey from her fingers. Then her gaze falls on the two picture frames. She wanted to move them; the kitchen isn't a good place for photos, but Erich doesn't want them in the bedroom.

A layer of grease has settled on the frames and glass and there's a thin layer of dust clinging to it that cannot be wiped off. Maja reaches for a package wrapped in tissue paper on the windowsill and lays it on the table, the thin paper sticking to her fingers. She holds her hands under the tap, dries them carefully on the tea towel before taking the picture frames off the wall and laying them in front of her on the table. She looks at her mother, her eyes small from laughing, looks at herself as a small child reaching a thin arm towards her mother so that she can catch her hand. There's a house in the other picture with hollyhocks, shrubs nestled grey on grey against the house walls, against the boards really. Her mother is standing in the foreground, aged four, wearing a lace-trimmed dress; she's laughing and holding a stick high in the air. Maja points her finger at the child's silhouette.

After a while she turns the frame over and bends the metal clips up. On the back of the picture of her mother in front of her parents' house, the year and place are written in faded Latin script, in her mother's writing.

Maja takes a pencil out of the table drawer and writes on the back of the second photo. Mama and I, she stumbles here – she doesn't know the date or place. She underlines the words, once, twice, then unpacks the new picture frames, lays the photos face-down on the glass, presses the metal clips closed and hangs the picture frames on the wall. She crumples the tissue paper and throws it onto the pile of newspapers beside the fridge, opens the fridge door, looking to see if there is any fruit there, then goes over to the kitchen window and tilts it open. The curtains wave gently in the draught; a window of the house opposite reflects the sun so that Maja is dazzled through the thin fabric.

Then, she's going to spend the day alone, dwell on her thoughts, answer no questions and ask none.

She pours cold water into her tea and drinks it in one long swallow. She packs apples, her bathing suit, a towel and a water bottle into a rucksack and, still standing there, puts the last morsel of bread in her mouth and calls to Erich that she is going now. She lets the door close noisily.

Someone has left brochures on the doormat. The first-floor neighbour always opens the door if someone rings; she knows all the leaflet distributers as well as the postman and if someone is out the postman leaves packages with her. This neighbour enjoys ringing on doorbells to hand them over in the evenings. Her eyes wander restlessly about as she stands on the threshold, looking to see if there is anything new in the flat, if she can spot something unusual that would be worth thinking about. Maja picks up the leaflets – Never wash your car again. Just call me, printed on a cheaply copied piece of paper. There are advertisements for beer, and a new clothes' shop. Maja opens the door again, throws the sheets with the wastepaper; Erich is sitting on the balcony looking at a magazine. I'm leaving my phone here, she calls. Do you hear, I'm going now.

Erich gets to his feet and comes into the hall.

You're still here, he says.

I'm going now, says Maja, leaving the phone on the shelf under the mirror. Whenever she is alone, she wants peace, she wants to go for a cycle, until she can hear her own pulse, until she can't do any more.

See you later, says Erich.

See you later, says Maja. Her sandals clatter loudly on the stairs. Maja clenches her toes so that the soles don't hammer so hard on the greasy pavement. The stairwell is cool with the only light falling from above. On the ground floor Maja turns the cellar light switch on. The walls are damp; you can't store anything here, only stuff you'd be happy to throw away at some stage. Maja keeps her bike in their cellar compartment anyway, at least it will rust less quickly there than outside. Like most people in the building, Erich leans his bike against the wall, locking it to the bars of the cellar window. Erich's bicycle chain is rusty and someone has taken the bell, but it's better than carrying it down the steep, partially cracked steps, Erich thinks. When they come home together, he always goes ahead and is already sitting in the kitchen when she closes the door behind her a few minutes later.

One of the two lightbulbs is broken; in the dim light Maja bangs her shin against a ladder that has fallen over. Tears spring into her eyes. She feels her leg: dry, no blood but the area is throbbing, burning. She presses her hand on it and the throbbing lessens. Maja shoves the ladder a little to one side, goes to her cellar compartment and tries to stick the key into the padlock. It is so dark that she can't do it. She feels for the little keyhole, holds her fingernail against the hollow and runs the key along her nail until it reaches the groove. Before turning the key, she bends down, touches her leg again and feels the bump. It's so quick, not even a minute and already her skin is bulging, burning. Maja dabs it with spit, opens the lock and pushes her bike out of the cellar compartment. Her front wheel is almost completely flat and she has to search for the pump which she finds right at the back. Clamping it onto the carrier, she carries the bike up the stairs and leans it against the wall. A door slams somewhere in the house. Maja hears raised voices, a man and his wife as the row penetrates into the stairwell. The sentences reach Maja strangely distorted, almost soft. The door closes again, more softly this time and one of them comes down the stairs. It's the man. He says hello and smiles as he passes Maja.

She pumps up the tyres; we should smoke less, she thinks. Something is wrong with this sentence or she would have forgotten it long ago, but it stood out from other sentences, hanging on the word we and the future.

We should smoke less, Maja whispers the sentence to herself, in rhythm with the in and out of the bicycle pump.

When she is ready, she leaves the pump on the letter box, pushes the heavy house door open and wheels the bike out onto the street.

The music from the radio can still be heard and a few houses down someone is playing the piano, running faultlessly up and down scales. As a child, she had wanted to learn an instrument, violin or piano, like the other girls in school whose parents brought them to the neighbouring village for music lessons once a week.

Maja looks down the street; the little café on the corner is open already but there's no one there yet. The waitress is wiping the tables with a cloth, putting out ashtrays and sticking ice-cream menus and price lists into their plexiglass holders. The café owner rolls out the striped awning; he's finding the winding hard work and is sweating. Rivulets run from the big plant pots, across the pavement and into the gutter. Maja gets onto her bike, says hello in passing, turns right and now the sun is in her face. She should have taken a hat, she never thought of it, but she doesn't want to turn around again. She feels only the airflow; the leaves on the trees are hanging motionless from the branches. The air in the city can stand still as if it were compressed violently between the houses, fastened onto something, and you had to cut your way through it, every step an effort. Maja can't remember ever having to move through standing air in the village. Only in the weedy, overgrown hollow by the stream where she and Fini always got their legs scratched; down there the heat often lay heavy on the ground, smelling sweet and almost bewitching.

Maja stands on the pedals, finding progress increasingly difficult, and the bike isn't steering properly. She looks at the wheel – it is almost flat again. She moves to the pavement and dismounts. This is pointless. She'll have to mend the tyre later; there must be a repair kit somewhere in the cellar. She takes the lock off the carrier and chains the bike to a lamp post. Now what, she is furious, blue sky, hours of perfect sunshine, a day to make the most of and do something to remember. And now she's standing there with a packed rucksack and a broken bike, on her own, even though she does have Erich. The sun burns down on her hair; there's a car on the other side of the street with its windows open. Paolo Conte singing, the driver wearing nothing but a bikini and a red hairband tied around her ponytail. She's tapping in time on the steering wheel and the passenger gazes at Maja as she stows the key in her rucksack. She takes out her purse and counts the coins. There's enough to sit in a café, to have an ice cream. That is what she will do. If she can't have the lake, she can have an ice cream, then a walk through the old city, climb into the fountain in her bare feet, listen in to people's conversations and try to understand what the tourists are saying.

She doesn't have to wait at the crossing as the light is green, and she walks across the zebra stripes. As a woman hurries past her, her heel sticks in the soft rubber casing around the tram tracks. Her bare foot hovers in the air for a moment, then she puts it down so as not to lose her balance, just the tips of her toes and hurriedly picks up the shoe, pulls it on again and continues as if nothing had happened, purposeful and elegant.

The sun burns on the tarmac and sun umbrellas and awnings can be seen on balconies, no people. Maja exhales as she goes through the archway, turns right over the cobblestones into the shade of the laneway. A stone skitters into her sandal, boring into the sole of her foot. She bends to remove it, getting dizzy as she straightens up again; she hasn't drunk enough, just a cup of tea in the morning. She leans against the wall of a house, takes a few steps towards the entrance, and sits down on the bottom step. The door is open, it smells of cellar and cool air blows over her skin. Black spots dance before her eyes and she pulls out her water bottle, takes a drink and pours a little water down her neck. A man in a light suit stops in front of her, bending towards her.

I'm okay, Maja says before he can ask, she looks at him and tries to smile. He has a little scar above the bridge of his nose and Maja's eyes fix on it.

Did you hurt yourself? the man asks, looking at Maja's leg.

It's not that bad, says Maja, even though she would like to say yes, yes, look after me, help me up, ask me how it happened and why, reach out your arm to me so that I can lean on it, so that I can lay my head against your shoulder for a minute.

But Maja pushes herself up off the step and brushes off her skirt.

Thank you, she says, beginning to follow with another sentence; then she notices a woman on the corner watching the two of them, a woman in a dark dress and high heels. Maja swallows her answer with a cough, the man wishes her a pleasant day and goes on. The woman hooks onto him, asks him something; he gestures something with his hand. Maja watches the couple until they turn onto a side street.

She is still dizzy, but the black spots have disappeared. She walks slowly, stopping in front of the window displays. The tourist shops are the only ones open; a few tourists take pictures of each other in front of a wild boar made of straw. Just behind it is an entrance to an inner courtyard where there's a rustling fountain and flower barrels with palm trees around the walls. Every summer, tables are arranged here with a bar as an improvised outdoor café. Waitresses in long green aprons carry cakes around the corner. Maja sits at a free table in the shade, reads the drinks menu and orders pineapple juice with ice.

There's a dark green bench between two palms at the opposite wall; Maja remembers the bench at the end of the walk she had once done with Erich that had ended unexpectedly as if they had forgotten to go on. Maja had closed her eyes, breathing in the smell of late summer, her skin warm from the sun. She had felt Erich's arm in hers but couldn't help thinking about what it would be like to share this bench with someone else. With Bert. Or with the neighbour opposite who always lies on the sofa in the evenings with books or newspapers and goes to the fridge around nine or half past, standing in front of it for a while as if he can't decide what to take out. In summer when she sits on the balcony, she looks into his flat watching the way he reads, eats a piece of bread or a slice of sausage. Sometimes Erich sits with her, and they smoke and drink a glass of wine and then Maja looks at Erich and tells herself things aren't that bad, the way she is living. But that day, on the bench, she had placed her hand on Erich's knee, heard her heart beating, and said that maybe she needed a third life, sometime, nothing else. Erich had looked at her, shaken his head, asked no questions and made no response. They had stood up and gone back on the same gravel path in silence.

Maja lets her eyes wander around the inner courtyard as an elderly couple approaches the neighbouring table. The man draws his wife's chair back, its legs scraping on the stones so that Maja jolts in spite of herself. The woman sits down cautiously, places her handbag on the table, pulls out her reading glasses and reads the menu. The man disappears, returning after a couple of minutes. He lists out the cakes: strawberry tart, apple cake, cardinal slices, banoffee pie.

I wonder if she says apple cake now, Maja thinks. Drinking coffee and eating apple cake at the peak of a life spent together. Fini had always said, promise me that you will look for something better. They had shook each other's hands and promised.

Apple cake, says the woman, pointing to the menu.

Coffee and a glass of water, the same for you? she asks; the man nods, waves the waitress over and orders his wife's cake. Maja imagines tasting the cake in the woman's place, the fork in her wrinkled hand, how she would spear it piece by piece, how content she would be with coffee and cake and a husband who would order them for her.

A dove flutters low over the tables and the old couple duck their heads; the man turns around and faces Maja. Something in his expression reminds her of Marek, perhaps the way he had moved his head. She hasn't thought of Marek for a long time; she sometimes asks Fini about him when they chat on the phone. The way he used to tell her fairy tales. And she would tell him about the Firebird and crafty Jemelia. He wanted to hear these stories over and over again, and together they would think up new tasks for Jemelia, sending him off, still lying on his warm stove, to faraway lands and strange, wild animals.

How she was allowed to sit on Marek's lap. Sometimes he stroked her hair or her cheek with his rough hand which always smelled a little of onions. She leaned against him, her back against his chest as he jigged his knees up and down and they would remain sitting like that for a while even after the story was over. She thought of how she had found no way of moving from fairy tales to adult conversation. Maja's place had moved from Marek's lap to the corner bench; then this shame had confused her, this taciturnity, the boredom she suddenly felt as she listened to him. How their intimate closeness had given way to a feeling of oppression she could rarely shake off. In the end she used to just stay at the garden fence and exchange a few banalities with him. She pitied him too because hardly anyone else ever visited him and she had seen how his eyes would light up as soon as she entered his house.

Maja rubs her shin where the bump has turned blue. The couple at the next table finish their coffee; they have pushed their empty cake plates aside. They are making plans for the coming week and there are long pauses between sentences as if everything being said had a special meaning.

Someone has thrown an empty drinks bottle in Maja's bicycle basket. She leans the bike beside the lamp post. The saddle is warm even though it is in the shade. It had been a long day – she had sat at the edge of the fountain, watched people, and in the afternoon, she had climbed the hill in the park. She fell asleep in the shadow of a beech tree and had even dreamed disjointedly until she was awoken by a dog barking. On the way back, she clambered over the edge of the fountain and waded through the knee-deep water until her skin was red with cold.

Maja bends down; the front tyre is completely flat now but she gets on the bike nevertheless and tries to cycle a few metres before realizing that she will ruin the wheel rim if she continues, so she dismounts and pushes. Her feet are still cool from the fountain, and she decides to take the longer route through the park. She thinks about Erich, wondering if he is still sitting on the balcony, if he had gone out, even to buy cigarettes or perhaps gone for a beer somewhere, if he had looked at the clock or thought of her. If she had brought her phone, she could have rung him to ask if he would like to meet her in the café on the corner. A glass of white wine would be nice, Maja thinks, maybe they could go there together, yes, she will suggest that to him.

The lights are on in some windows and dusk is falling over the roofs of the houses. Maja opens the door. The lights are on throughout the flat; Erich emerges from the kitchen.

There you are, he says.

Yes, says Maja. Suddenly she is uncertain whether she should ask Erich, she can't read his expression, something is different.

Were you crying? she asks.

Erich turns around, doesn't answer. There's a smell of tomatoes and onions. Erich has been cooking, a tea towel hanging from the belt of his trousers. Maja puts her hands on his shoulders; she wants to turn him around to face her, but he dodges out of her grasp and runs his hands over his face.

It's alright, he says.

Maja puts her rucksack down beside the door. Erich turns to her.

Will we go for a drink? he asks and Maja nods.

I wanted to ask you too, she says, looking into Erich's eyes. He holds her gaze and puts money into his trousers pocket.

Have you the key? he asks.

Yes, says Maja, I do.

There are lemon candles burning on the tables, a waiter is serving. He has a black ring in one ear through which you can see the skin of his neck. His eyebrows are plucked, and Maja cannot keep her eyes off them with their precisely drawn lines on his almost boyish-looking face. Maja orders a glass of white wine, Erich a beer. They watch the people strolling past on the street below, a couple pushing a buggy, the child still awake, crying. The mother bends down, strokes her, speaking comforting words and as they have gone past the tables, she straightens up and walks beside the buggy. Maja can hear the child still crying. She leans her head back; the awnings have long

since been rolled up and she is looking into the sky. The
end of August is the time for most shooting stars. But
she can see only a half moon above the streetlights and
only four stars. Erich drinks half his glass in one gulp and
clears his throat.

Fini rang, he says.

How is she? Maja asks.

Good, says Erich, but Marek.

Maja puts down her glass, her heart beginning to beat
faster; she can feel it in her throat. A dryness in her mouth
and throat as if she had drunk sand, not wine. She coughs
and looks Erich in the eye.

Yes? she asks, what's up with him?

Marek is dead, says Erich. This afternoon. I'm
supposed to tell you.

The wine glass has clouded over, and a drop runs
slowly down the outside, leaving an irregular trail. Maja
stops the drop with her finger, stares at Erich who looks
away fixing his eyes on the tabletop and the sides of his
mouth jerk.

Why did he cry, she asks herself, why.

VI
Room Three

Though she has long since turned off the engine, Maja is sitting up straight, clutching the steering wheel as if she wanted to take off on a winding road at any moment. After a while she pulls up the zipper on her jacket, feels behind the seat for her handbag, pulls it forward, takes out her cigarette packet and, turning it in her hand, looks through the wet windshield before putting the cigarettes away again.

Bert is sitting in the back seat with his eyes closed, Erich standing in the rain a few steps away, smoking.

What difference does it make! he had roared. Tell me what, what is it you want!

She hadn't been able to stand it anymore, Erich's picking at his fingernails, scratching his underarms, the constant throat-clearing without saying anything, the way he threw his head back as he did so, his harrumphs sounding like a nervous bark.

What do you care! It's got nothing to do with you, he said, avoiding her eyes as he spoke.

Nothing matters! Maja shouted, I've had enough, couldn't either of you at least open your mouth!

Maja had to brake hard as the road had become potholed, and she had seen the roadworks sign too late. Erich reached his arm for the handbrake, his breath hissing.

The country road wove through fallow fields, occasional signposts pointing towards a village or a guesthouse. The rain intensified and Maja wanted to turn on the windscreen wipers, but they wouldn't move. Erich bent forward and lifted the lever up and down.

Stop that, do you think it's my fault that they're not working? she cried and, pushing Erich away with her elbow, she steered the car into a meadow, turned off the engine, shouting at Erich until he opened the car door and got out, until the damp air penetrated the interior, until Bert leaned over the passenger seat and closed the door again, laying his hand on Maja's shoulder, nothing more, just the weight of his hand on her shoulder.

Marek's hand on her child's hand, just before she left, her mute farewell. Her fingers on his embroidered tablecloth, on the yellow-bird beaks, on the green, blue, and red feathered heads, fingers she couldn't keep still when Marek told her his fairy tales. She pushed her fingers through the holes on the tablecloth border and they had red marks when she pulled them out again. Marek who never scolded her, who knew she was all ears to him, who let her fidget and stroked her cheek occasionally and who was always there when she knocked on his door.

She can remember every bird and every stray thread of that tablecloth. But Marek's face. The birthmark on his chin, the grey hair that was always a little too long on his neck, his dark incisor-tooth, the light-brown spots in his eyes, the face on the photograph she took out of the envelope. Fifty-fifty, the letters in white touch-up pen raised off the paper. Maja sees the face in the photo, she only ever sees that photograph face, as if she had never known any other.

The rain hammers on the car roof, leaving trails on the windows. At irregular intervals a passing car lights up the interior, the open glove-box, the dropped sunshade on the passenger side, the two tiny plastic roses on a pearl knot hanging from the ignition key. A lorry slows down, stops for a moment, and then drives on.

Maja watches Bert in the rear-view mirror. He's crouched into the corner, headphones on, eyes closed as if none of this had anything to do with him. As if he couldn't be seen as long as he didn't see anything himself. His chest rises and falls regularly but she doesn't think he's asleep; he couldn't fall asleep that quickly, she thinks, in the space of just a few minutes.

I don't fight with people I don't love, says Maja but Bert doesn't hear her. Maja reaches her arm back, knocks on Bert's leg, and he opens his eyes and takes off the headphones.

I don't fight with people I don't love, Maja says again, and Bert answers, that's alright. He looks at Maja, waits, but she doesn't say anything else, just shakes her head slowly. A little jolt goes through his body, but he pulls his half-outstretched arm back and replaces his headphones. Maja can hear very faint percussion and a hint of guitar.

It was Bert who came to her that time when she was standing lost in the factory, knowing nobody, and not knowing what exactly she had to do.

I'll bring you there and you can take the bus tomorrow, Erich had said over a hasty breakfast, and she was there, standing on the forecourt almost an hour too early, without stockings, in shoes that were too high and wearing the short dress that Erich liked so much.

Eventually she had waited by the conveyer belt in a white coat and white clogs with her hair in a hairnet that scratched her hairline, as Bert came in through a side entrance. Instead of offering his hand, he had put an arm around her as if he knew her, as if she didn't know him only from Erich's stories.

I'll show you around, don't worry, it's not difficult, he had said, by afternoon you will know your way around, you'll see.

So, you're Erich's best friend, she had said, I had imagined you completely different.

His soft round body, his round face with laughter lines around his eyes. His feet turned outwards as he walked, his eyelids blinking as he spoke. He listened to Erich's music, went around with him for nights on end and had sorted this job for her.

Thank you, said Maja.

Bert grinned.

He hadn't moved from her side and had patiently explained the work systems to her, more often than was necessary. And when she was no longer making mistakes and, together with the other young women, could check the orange-coloured cartons: medicines, disposable syringes, bandaging materials, no longer asking herself who really needed so much Halcion or Tramal, he had continued to check on her regularly anyway and sometimes suggested going to the city centre with her to show her the best cafés and pubs. If she wanted, they could go to the cinema together, he said. He invited her for a beer after work, in the city centre, where she didn't know her way around yet; Erich could join them too.

Erich hugged her from behind, clapped Bert on the shoulder; okay, little guy, he said, watching Maja as he said it and they drank beer until it was getting bright again.

Maja had got into the habit of giving Bert some of her bread at lunchtime because he never had enough with him. They sat together on the steps in the backyard and Bert offered her a cigarette.

Tell me something, he said, and they remained sitting on the steps until the half-hour was over. The way Bert listened to her when they sat beside each other, the way he looked at her, looking away quickly as soon as their eyes met.

Maja watched Bert through the glass pane as he walked along between the rows of tall shelves carrying and stacking boxes. Sometimes, when they were short-staffed, he would come in with the checklists and stand so close to her that their arms touched. And she got used to wishing Bert a pleasant evening outside the cloakroom, hanging her white work coat in her locker, standing in front of the mirror to release her hair from a ponytail, putting on lipstick, swapping her clogs for high heels and, once outside, slipping her arm through Erich's. He was always there five minutes early, moving from one foot to the other as he waited.

On Fridays the three of them would usually go to Bert's place and he would cook noodles or a stew for everyone, and then they would go out, Maja and Erich in front and Bert behind or Bert would walk ahead with Maja with Erich following and, if there was enough space in the pedestrian zone, or in the middle of the night, Maja would go in the middle, her arm hooked onto Erich, brushing against Bert as they walked.

One time they had entered a narrow side street and stopped in front of a shuttered shop window.

Wait a moment, Maja had called, her hands on the shutter. Russian tea and a samovar with sweets strewn between them as though by coincidence. Right in front, up against the glass, stood a row of Matryoshka dolls, their faces towards Maja, seven dolls, seven tiny scenes from fairy tales on their chests, framed in a light-blue flowered pattern on a red background. Maja's palms began to sweat. Her Matryoshka, she had really had a Matryoshka, in the past; she hadn't thought about it in such a long time.

What is it, come on, come, Erich had called. Bert had remained standing beside Maja, looking through the shutters with her. Erich turned around, put his arm around Maja, turned her to face him and kissed her. Bert stood aside, waited, counted the dolls, and looked at the samovar.

Maja sees Erich coming back, a dark shadow with a vague outline, sees him hazily through the rain-soaked windscreen. He opens the car door, sits in, keeping his soaking jacket on, rolls down the window and looks at the front wheel that has sunk into the meadow.

Do you think we can get out of here again? he asks.

Maja pays no attention but turns on the little light beside the sunshade.

Bert? Do you hear me? Have you got the map with you? She calls back over her shoulder and Bert opens his eyes, reaches into his jacket pocket, and pulls out a much-folded sheet. He smooths it flat before offering it to Maja.

It's even in colour, says Maja, and on heavy paper. She runs her index finger over the pale-grey lines.

We'll drive on and look for a hotel.

They drive on slowly, in silence. Erich scrutinizes Maja out of the corner of his eye; the engine noise muffles the music emanating from Bert's headphones.

There are billboards along the roadside; a car overtakes them without indicating. Drops of water against the windscreen, a play of light from red rear lights and street lamps. Maja steps on the brakes, concentrating on the reflective posts along the side of the road. She can make out a warehouse, a broad entrance, a car park containing an articulated lorry and a small car with its sidelights on, then meadow again and a couple of trees. The rain intensifies. Erich swears.

There are signposts ahead, she says, perhaps they will show something.

Perhaps, Erich says, bobbing his knees up and down and drumming his fingers on his thighs.

Slow down, there are signposts, he says.

The windscreen is too wet for anyone to be able to decipher the letters. Maja switches on the hazard lights and stops at the side of the road. Erich gets out and runs through the headlight beam towards the signs.

Bert straightens up, pushing forward on the back seat, holding onto Maja's headrest. He takes off his headphones, inhales as if he wanted to say something but then Erich comes back and Bert lets his outstretched hand drop, asks Erich what he has found out and Erich says, yes, turn left in three hundred metres.

Maja is reminded of the three hundred metres that the three of them had driven on one of their first weekends together, when they had switched off the lights on the motorway, just because they could, because it was a full moon and there was nothing happening, and the motorway was dead straight and Maja had been happy because everything had seemed possible, everything.

The car park is full. There is a dance hall on the other side of the street; the bass booms outwards and blue-green light chains hang between two illuminated red hearts. Maja remains standing beside the car and closes her eyes. The afterimage of the country road, the rain-soaked windscreen, the distorted light of oncoming traffic plays on like a film behind her eyelids.

I'll be right there, she says.

Two men are standing beside the entrance of the hotel, chatting quietly and one offers the other a cigarette. As she passes them, Maja notices the bigger of the two looking her up and down.

Bert opens the door; the reception area is dark with only a weak ceiling-lamp spreading yellowish light. There's a dusty palm tree standing against the wall. Maja feels the leaves – they're plastic. Erich is standing in front of the price list, the television is on in the little room behind reception. Bert walks a few steps over and back. Erich clears his throat and Maja leans on the door, burying her hands in her jacket pockets. She feels as if she's forgotten something, fingers the car keys and lets them go again.

She hears a chair being moved back and the porter emerges. Bert goes up to the reception desk. You do the talking, Maja had said. There's some shooting on the television and the light in the back room flickers rapidly between bright and dark as the television images change.

There are three of us, Bert says. The porter looks from one to the other. Erich is the only one with an overnight bag. Bert is wearing his leather jacket with the pockets bulging.

Booked out, the porter answers, we only have a double room left, but Bert speaks to him quietly, mentions an emergency, a funeral, and siblings, offers him two bank notes and finally signs a form. Room three, first floor, Bert tells Maja and Erich after looking at the room key. He asks about directions and breakfast. Maja hears only fragments; she is too tired to follow the conversation. Erich shoulders his overnight bag and goes in front. The porter looks after them, shaking his head, and remains standing in reception until he hears Bert turn the key in the door.

The room is small and stuffy, and they don't turn the lights on because the street lights shine through the window. Maja opens both sides of the window and pulls at the zip of her handbag until she eventually manages to open it and take out her cigarettes.

Anyone got a match? she asks. Bert offers her his lighter, one with a topless woman on it – he always has lighters like this. Erich gets his from cafés. Maja looks at the breasts in the orange light of the street light, the half-open scarlet lips, and gives the lighter back. They smoke; Erich takes off his shoes and socks.

Don't walk barefoot on the carpet, Maja says but Erich puts both feet on the ground, remains sitting for a while, then hauls himself off the bed with feigned effort and goes into the bathroom, leaving the door open. Maja doesn't look but she hears the splashing, the toilet flushing, running tap. Then he comes behind her, laying a cold wet hand on her neck; she gasps, drawing air in through her nose and choking on the smoke.

Just leave her alone, says Bert, but Erich leaves his hand there and Maja doesn't defend herself.

Bert throws his butt out the window. Maja does the same. Erich runs his foot over Maja's shin even though he knows that the carpet disgusts her, and she shrinks from his touch.

Let's go to bed, she says, without looking at either of the two. The room is better than a night in the car, but she won't be able to sleep. She will hear Erich and Bert breathing, sudden loud snoring that will make her wince, she'll snap her fingers, but it won't do any good. She'll get up and go out into the corridor and stand at the window looking down on the backyard, hearing the hum of the air-conditioning, looking at the heavy-hanging clouds – she will have to lean halfway out the window to see them.

At some stage the bedroom door will open, and Bert will come out, lay an arm on Maja's shoulder, and ask why she puts up with Erich. And Maja will answer, I know, I know, Bert. She will lean both her hands on the stone windowsill to support herself, feeling its coolness. She will look at Bert and ask herself why he always has lighters like that, ones that don't suit him.

What do you think, who's going to be there? She will ask then in the silence and Bert will answer, I don't know, it's not important. And they will remain silent, and Bert will stroke Maja's back and she will let him. After a while his stroking will become slower, and he'll turn around and go back to bed.

Maja will sit on the windowsill and freeze, wishing that she had brought the duvet with her. She will close her eyes and think of Marek, about the day when he brought her the building bricks, the short conversation before she left, their farewell. About his rigidity which she couldn't read. About the sound of her steps on the gravel, the creak of the garden gate, the words he shouted after her.

Her heart had begun to race when Erich confided in her that Marek was his father and that he had discovered by coincidence and was forbidden to talk about it, that it had not been easy for him. His mother wanted to have peace in the village, and it would have changed nothing, absolutely nothing. That silence was not a lie – I didn't lie to you, hear me out! His mother could not have lived with Marek; their brief attempt had failed. Fini had a different father, and he didn't know any more, he didn't want to know any more.

Maja thinks how one story inserts itself into another, right from her earliest childhood, also that she can't change any of it.

The squeak of the bedroom door will startle Maja and Erich will come out, ask her what she's doing there, and she'll tell him, nothing, I'm not doing anything, and Erich will go back into the room again and later Maja will too.

Eventually the night will be over, and they will get up. They will be alone in the breakfast room apart from the long-distance lorry driver and they will say very little, just perhaps which is the best road to take. Maja will drink coffee and Bert will say she should eat something; she needs to eat, and he will butter her a piece of bread and Maja will nibble at it and pour herself another cup of coffee.

Erich will get up from the table quickly; he needs a cigarette, he will say. After a while, Maja and Bert will go out to the car and Erich won't be there; there'll be a note stuck behind the windscreen wiper.

Go on your own, I can't go, Erich will have written.

Maja will look at Bert who will press his lips together until they are almost white; the truck will be gone. Bert will look Maja in the eye and take the car keys from her outstretched hand.

VII
Mother Holle

I remember a light that dazzles and confuses me because at night everything is dark, and everyone sleeps: sleep my little angel, sleep, people sleep, animals sleep, the bear and the fox and the dog, go to sleep now.

A light and a big room are what I remember. I don't know how long I'm there – the adults are trying to hide their agitation from me.

I remember a golden button, perhaps part of a police uniform, a red stripe on a dark-blue sleeve.

I see a bit of the sky through the skylights. It changes from black to grey. I don't know if I am sitting up or put lying down, if someone brings me something to drink, tries to explain something to me or even sings me a song.

A memory trail of isolated images leads back to this night, arms that lift me out of the cot. Even though I must be too big for it already, I am unable to climb out on my own. Perhaps my mother didn't want me getting up at night and roaming through the house unnoticed. I do remember that my throat hurt from screaming, that I cried for my mother, and she didn't come. The hammering on the door, people talking at me, without me understanding them, people in uniforms standing around in my mother's bedroom, the smell of exhaust and cold smoke in a car. I remember that I turn around and try to bite the arms that are holding me.

The hilly landscape has softened into an endless plain like coloured rugs disappearing into the horizon. The sky pales gradually and Maja, seeing a swarm of birds, observes how they constantly change shape. She strokes her child and pulls her blanket straight. Anja's small warm body with the weight of her head on Maja's left arm, sometimes she twitches in her sleep.

The train moves slowly across a set of points. A disproportionately large building appears beyond the fields, concrete walls in the middle of nowhere, rusty fire escapes and small blank windows. The surface of the access road has broken down and weeds poke up between the cracks and while it's clear which is stronger, there's no signpost, no indication to see what has been vanquished by time here. As Maja passes by the walls she sees hundreds of rusty barrels, their labels no longer legible.

Behind the factory grounds are more fields, meadows, and derelict lots where weeds grow tall. A brown-green river whose water seems to stand still. A few women are sitting in a circle in one field, a tractor stopped aslant in the furrows. Occasional trees flash by and a row of poplars casts long shadows.

Maja tries to open the window. Carefully, so as not to waken Anja, she reaches her arm up and pulls the aluminium handle. A narrow gap lets fresh air in. It is cooler than Maja had expected and carries the smell of freshly cut grass into the compartment.

The train is moving very slowly now, approaching a level-crossing. A white car and a horse and cart are waiting there, and the cart driver has got down. He's wearing a colourful pullover and a jacket; he sticks something into his mouth, looking back at the engine.

In a few hours, in the middle of the night, they will pass the final border. Maja has the warnings in her ears and the horror stories: anyone could be threatened with hostility or face groundless accusations, sometimes people are even detained for no reason. The surname on their passport might not be accepted or they could be questioned. She doesn't want to believe these stories and yet a steadily growing anxiety prevents her from sleeping. She thinks of soldiers walking up and down on the roof of the train for hours, checking the engine, using torches to look under every seat, rummaging through every bag and every case, asking questions, taking an unbearable length of time to scrutinize every passport, or read visas, and about the minutes that pass until they stamp the documents. She imagines the fearful faces of those people forcibly removed from the train and brought into a little hut with dirt-smeared windows, where they stand under cold neon-lights, left in doubt about what is wanted from them. Their children remain sitting in the train, cowering close together, a bigger one holds the smallest by the hand; they lower their eyes, look at the soldiers' boots, remaining silent because they have been forbidden to utter even a word.

They will leave us in peace, I tell myself. I catch myself moving my lips as I do so. We just want to look for a house and to see where my mother grew up, and my grandmother.

I stretch out my legs; we are alone in the compartment. The last stop was hours ago. The train takes more and more time to cover ever shorter stretches. Something rattles and I let my eyes wander through the compartment looking for a loose hook or a hanging bit of plastic. The screws on the interior finishings are loose; the top corner of a panel is warped, the hollow space a hiding place for cigarettes or vodka perhaps.

I wonder if my grandfather was a smuggler, travelling across the border at weekends to get rid of his goods as quickly as possible on the platform, and then take the next train home. Would he have counted his money on the journey home, was it worth it for him, if he was caught? I wonder if my grandmother waited for him at the stop or at home, would she see him coming from afar, would he lay his hand on her rounding belly. I wonder if he used the money to buy milk and eggs, so that my mother could grow in Grandmother's belly.

I imagine us getting off the train in the morning, the effort of getting to the bus station, and I wonder how busy it will be at this time. The rising sun hints that it's going to be a hot day and there's still birdsong to be heard, swallows that have nested under a roof. I will need a little time to get my bearings and will read a few sentences from my bit of paper to find the correct bus, feeling ashamed that I didn't learn the sentences by heart. The bus driver won't help us to get on. We will take our seats and I will offer a few roubles at the front like the other passengers. The journey will take a while, leaving the city again, on bumpy country roads, past disused railway stations. I will be hoping that Anja stays quiet, that the other passengers will not scrutinize us too obviously, and I can't wait to get the final kilometres behind me.

We are the only ones getting out here and there's nobody there to stare at us: a woman with a small child, hardly any luggage and certainly not a local. The bus stop is unmarked, or the bus driver has simply dropped us at the side of the road. I open out Anja's blanket, she cries, and I have to put her down for a moment while I unfold the buggy. Then I take her on my arm, rocking her, before placing her in the buggy and hanging our only bag on the handles. It's almost as if we were on a day trip to visit an old aunt.

Foreignness can be hidden in a small bag, but the child's buggy will attract attention because it obviously comes from somewhere far away.

Maja is surprised at how fast the colour of the sky changes, how quickly darkness falls over the landscape, how gloomy it is. Anja has woken up and Maja gives her a drink, but she still won't stop crying. She hums her a song, holding her lips against Anja's ear, inventing a melody, two or three notes, two up and one down. She hums and rocks, closes her eyes and it seems as if she is looking at herself there, as if she were sitting on the red-upholstered bench beside a woman who is trying to calm a small child. A mother, a child, and a grandmother too. She wonders if Grandmother's eyes were sometimes as red as Marek's. Did she stand at the window, seeing fiery rafters instead of the freshly painted boards? In her ears did the cawing of a rook become the scream of a mother who hunted her children into the forest? Go away! Go, run, run! Standing at the edge of the forest, did she see the darkness between the trees that was supposed to save the children? Did she see a mother crouched whimpering over the dead cow? Did she see cellars, oxcarts, soldiers' boots, black eyes, swarms of flies behind the house?

Did she put vodka and berry liqueur on the table in the evenings, pouring a glass for Grandfather and did she speak out a wish into the silence of the room, then raise both glasses and drink the vodka herself after the liqueur?

That is my thumb That shakes down a plum.

I hold a thumb out to Anja; she sticks it in her mouth and scratches my skin with her little teeth.

That is the thumb, my thumb, look, my thumb for you.

The weeks in the home, all shrivelled up into a few images. I remember a colourful room with children running around. An open terrace door, where I'm standing watching the children and looking into the garden. A blonde girl sits in a sandpit digging a hole and, at the same time, trying to tell a smaller girl sitting in the sand not to eat it – I can't see either face or hair, just two fat little legs in white tights, partially covered in sand. A bigger child takes me by the hand, pulls me into a corner and presses a doll onto my lap. The doll has eyes that open and close and I move them around, feeling the plastic eyelids and touching the pupils.

And then fear rises in me as I am brought to the sick bay. I stand in the small white room which smells of disinfectant; I'm standing in front of a doctor, on my own. He pulls up my vest to listen to my chest. His grey moustache hangs over his upper lip, he has a deep voice and rough hands. A cold floor under my feet. He puts me on a weighing scales, looks into my mouth and my ears. I don't know what he wants with me.

The matron of the children's home has long blonde hair; her front teeth leave marks on her chapped lower lip, and she has freckles on her nose. Did she press toys into my hand? And then words: ball, doll, car, pronounced very slowly and loudly, looking at me and frowning as I tried to shape my mouth around them? Did these new words sneak into my sleep over the fairy tales and songs, the sentences my mother had laid down here.

My first years: a playground, I'm sitting on a wooden horse with the taste of apple juice on my tongue. A red raincoat made of heavy rubber; its oval wooden buttons have to be pushed through loops. A dark-green mat, a wooden door, a pack of cards on the floor, I'm sitting in the corner bending the playing cards in my hands. I see my mother's slender fingers, her hand, her hand over and over again. It is as if I had never looked at her face. This hand covers me up when I lie in bed with a high fever. My poor angel, I know that's what she said; I know and yet I can't hear her voice. I hear the sentence in my head as if I were saying it myself: my poor angel, my poor angel.

Everything has translated itself and nothing is missing that would not have been lost otherwise but, somehow, it doesn't feel familiar; the mother and child words of the feathery cave lie scattered somewhere, as if Mother Holle had shaken them too hard, as if a slit had appeared, letting the feather-soft secrecy tumble out.

The child has fallen asleep. Maja spreads out the blanket beside her on the bench seat, lays Anja on it and covers her with her jacket. She draws the curtains across the window, switches off the main light and turns the reading lamp on. She hears voices in the corridor, two men and a woman. The words sizzle past the compartment; the people seem upset. The woman begins to cry and one of the men lowers his voice, then the second one.

The sound of the wheels on the tracks, the curtains sway gently. Maja takes paper and a pen out of her travel bag, leans her head against the window, watching her sleeping child. Her blonde curls above her forehead, the little fist at her lips. Who did she get these curls from, she writes, where did she get these toenails, that grow curving downwards, so different to mine.

Let me write to you so that the words do not get tangled, and the sentences flow properly. Or else I can throw the paper away so it can dissolve in the waterfilled ditches, in the marsh, so it can catch in the weeds clawing with yellow brightness onto the railway bank. So I can fold it up and so it is possible for you to roam smoothly through my words.

So that my voice is in your head and not in your ear.

Your voice in my ear, do you remember? That night when you sang a song for me, just before dawn. You only wanted to ask me if I knew the title and then you sang the first verse and while I was still shaking my head you thought, good, you don't want it any other way. And you hadn't sung it wrong; I recognized the song straightaway, but I told you, you had to sing on. From those first couple of beats came the whole song, soft and yet clear, and I was astonished at how high your voice sounded when you sang. I laid my head on your chest and whispered, don't stop, Bert, don't stop, and you really did sing me all the verses, tapping your free hand on the green fitted-sheet, the other hand stroking my back in time to the music.

I don't know if it was then or later that I was lying beside you with my fingers in your hand. You just held them, nothing more. First, I stroked the back of your hand with my thumb because I felt I had to do something and eventually I did become calmer, as if the way you were lying there could be taken for granted, your head on your bent arm, your legs on top of the duvet, because you were too warm under it; your warmth had transferred to me. At some stage, I too stopped moving and looked at the play of lights on the bare wall, created by the lights of passing cars coming through the cracks in the blinds. Strips of light chasing each other without ever touching.

We were both on this green-covered mattress. You had disappeared into the bathroom for a moment after we had got to your flat and I heard the washing machine door give a loud click and then you pushed past me, picked up a couple of bits of clothing from the chair and threw them behind the sofa. You pulled the sheet out of the wash basket and quickly spread it over the mattress. You only switched on the small lamp, and we didn't speak another word; you didn't even ask how I felt, and I was happy about that.

And then I lost my courage, Bert. Changing this possibility of having a family into reality and being invited to family celebrations by your relations. Having to shrug or shake my head. No, I don't know where my father lives. Yes, it's interesting that I've forgotten my own language, but I don't speak Belarusian anymore, no, unfortunately, I can't even say a sentence for you. A few words, but they are learned quickly. They roll out of my mouth easily, I admit, and they really sound as if they were cut from a recording, spoken by a Belarusian.

The feeling of a language is the only inheritance that has remained with me.

Your hand, that you laid on my rounded belly. How I explained that I cannot live with you, at least not yet.

And despite that, you still helped me to find a new flat and carry the heavy desk down to the cellar.

What do I need a desk for, I said to the landlady, and I took down the dark curtains, opened the side windows and unpacked my boxes.

The Matryoshka you gave me sits on the windowsill. I took it apart and stuck the smallest doll in my jacket pocket. The doll doesn't rattle when you shake it, and you'd hardly notice that the smallest one is missing.

I wanted to call you before I set off but I was afraid you would talk me out of making this journey.

At least leave Anja here, I'll look after her, you

know, I could mind her well, you know that. That's what you would have said but I would have got on the train nevertheless, and would still have brought Anja with me, along with a bad conscience, feeling I had thrown your advice to the wind and fearing you would have been right.

Anja sucks at Maja's thumb. Maja leans back, stretches out her legs and closes her eyes. Images of the landscape pull past her, pine woods separated from the meadows as if with a ruler, tight rows of tall trees where you would immediately become disorientated, and which you only need to follow to find your way out again. They give way to thousand-year-old forests lying on the land like thick bison hide, covered with scars, cut through in long swathes by man-high fences and kilometres of barbed wire.

Babushkas stand on the forlorn platforms to sell their mushrooms and berries. Blue sky over the tired hands of the old women, their eyes full of sadness and fear and resignation too, and their hands again, stuffing money into their pockets, a few notes that they have got for their mushrooms to exchange for wood or coal so as not to freeze in winter. Men wait for them at home, their eyes watery from cheap vodka; children, who are playing alone in the dirt, wear clothes from charity parcels and perhaps they remember a summer when they were allowed to stay with friendly people hundreds of kilometres away so they could recover their strength. Mothers who long since stopped worrying whether they are allowed to give their children mushrooms and berries from the forests or not.

And behind the villages, these endless fields of wheat spreading gold over the soft hills, moving like waves in the wind.

I let the movement of the train rock me back into the possibility of a childhood, into a childhood that might have been, into the possible memory of a grandmother awaiting the arrival of my mother and myself, who's been standing waiting at the fence for hours already, all preparations for our arrival finished hours ago. A dark-blue enamelled pot filled with almond biscuits sits on the kitchen table; there's borscht bubbling on the stove, gherkins, dried mushrooms, potatoes, onions and homemade bread in the larder. The wooden floorboards are covered with soft rugs; there are hangings with sunflowers and onion-steepled churches on the walls and, in the living room, the main room of the house, a framed photo of Mother and me. Presents are laid out ready on the only bed (Grandmother is going to sleep in the living room, although Mother protests about that): a Matryoshka, the most beautiful one Grandmother could lay her hands on and, beside her, a doll with eyes that open and close, hand-embroidered blouses, a little woollen jacket and tablecloths embroidered on long winter evenings, their patterns of entwined flowers inspired by the filigree of frost tracery on the frozen windows.

There's a fragrance in the house, emanating from things that everyone who has ever been in a Belarusian house recognizes immediately, a fragrance that can only be described through things. My grandmother has tried to banish all the flies and has drawn the curtains over the window. The fly curtain at the house door with its bright strings of beads rattles in the light wind. The hens can be heard from inside the living room, the soup bubbling, the dog running over and back on the length of his chain or chewing on a bone. The gentle rustle of fabric when The grandmother strokes the child. It is so quiet that the stroking can be heard.

I would have hidden behind my mother and a few seconds would have passed before my grandmother enveloped her daughter in her arms as tears ran down both their cheeks and I would not have known what to do. And then, after a long while, my grandmother would have turned to me and carefully taken my face in her raw hands, shaking her head as if she couldn't believe she was at last allowed to see her grandchild.

Many stories have touched mine; they change and blend and sometimes I cannot even say where one ends and the next begins. I have made them my own, borrowed them, thought onwards, too far perhaps, and wrapped them around me like a camouflage coat; but now, now I want to move into my own story, to hold the village and valley of my childhood up against the landscape that remained concealed from me.

Listen Bert, I am missing the stories about uncles and aunts that people tell over and over at Christmas. About the cousin who lost his way at night and was drawn onto the moors by the will-o'-the-wisp and only escaped by pure chance. About the great uncle who remained standing so long in front of a great-aunt's house that she took pity on him and took him for her husband. About a grandfather who laboured, day-in day-out, in a brick factory and afterwards on the potato field where one day he found God's fingers or fulgurite. The family tells how he dug up the glassy formations and wanted to carry them into the village, but nobody could do that without incurring bad luck; he fell over, broke his shoulder and the fingers of God broke at the same time, crumbled to smithereens, and the grandfather fell silent and only spoke of it shortly before his death. And then the unspoken secrets, the things you are not even allowed to think about. The hush, when a child asks, it's nothing for you to be concerned about yet, and it is better for you to know nothing about it. Then the adults look at each other for a moment; everyone waits for someone else to start talking about something else, a thread that can weave the conversation onwards so that it can continue late into the evening.

In my memory is a silence. I remember a silent cold house where only the wooden floorboards murmured when my aunt moved around: you can't cut yourself a slice of the past; quiet, be quiet, be content with what you have.

Do not think that sitting in the train for days on end just to see a house that may not even be there any longer is nonsense. I need to see everything, everything that my mother saw, I want to feel how long this journey is, how the tapestry of sound changes in the compartment as we go through different countries. Anja is sleeping beside me and I'm holding her hand.

I cried after you rang me on my birthday. Your voice so near and the knowledge that I just had to sit on the bus to be with you in a few hours. The knowledge that you are thinking of me, and you haven't given up hope. And then this sentence again – look after yourself. The loveliest sentence that anyone can say. A soft sentence, you need to listen carefully and then it spreads out and swings and resonates; there is so much trust in it and more love than the word love itself could capture.

She's not called Babushka – she's Matryoshka. My aunt's words. Her voice in my head.

I can't peel the stories from my belly. I travel into a landscape and into a language that could also have been mine. I want to take away a background, before which something could have played out – a childhood, a summer, a visit. The image of a house my mother could have told me about, the image of a forest she could have wandered through as a child, the image of endless wheatfields where she could have hidden, the image of a rusty water pump, a cement road, a forlorn railway station where she stood forty years ago (and which no longer exists), full of hope and fear, with nothing but a little leather case beside her and carefully saved coffee for the soldiers on the border.

I hoped to encounter my mother tongue in dreams, even if I could not save any of it to bring forth into the day; I'm not even sure if people speak in dreams.

The house is still standing even if strangers live in it, it must still be standing. I will park my buggy behind a fence and take Anja in my arms, otherwise I will get stuck forever between cobblestones and hard-stamped earth. Only the main street is surfaced, and last night's rainwater lies in the potholes. I hear a dog barking, followed closely by the barks of other dogs, a bellowing and howling that lasts for several minutes. The streets are empty as we walk past grey wooden houses; some were painted years ago and flakes of yellow and pale-blue varnish hang from the planks on the weathered side. But there are hollyhocks growing in almost every garden, flowerbeds behind low fences, a bench in front of every house. An old man is cracking sunflower seeds with his teeth, spitting the shells at his feet, watching us. He calls something to his wife who doesn't hear him and throws a bucket of dirty water out on the street. I say hello but she says nothing, not even when I nod at her. The sky is steel-blue and the thunderclouds have vanished. The house faces onto a little pine forest. I am surprised that it is fenced but, as I come nearer, I see gravestones between the trees. I know there's no point in looking for my grandmother's grave here; she lies beside my grandfather far away, but nevertheless I open the gate and walk between mossy gravestones and the few standing wooden crosses scattered between them, seeming to tower randomly above the grass. The flowers belong to the living; the dead rest under soft green, untroubled by sprinkled water. I sit on a bench with Anja; there are sunflower seeds in the grass, and for me it is as if someone has arranged them in a pattern or letters that I cannot read. For a moment, I forget what I am looking for and stare at the lines, lifting my feet so that they do not tread on the sign. I'm making very little progress; it's already after midday, and I haven't reached the edge of the village.

When I want to leave the graveyard, I become aware of a smell like burnt herbs; I look around but can't spot anything. In the house opposite the curtains move, a shadow retreats back into the room.

Anja sits on my hip and I lay my cotton shawl over her head to shield her from the sun, but she immediately pulls the shawl down again to chew at it. I hear only my steps and Anja's soft slurping. The child is heavy on my arm; I change her to the other side and then I see the last house on the main street. As if someone had painted over the black and white photograph, it stands there, the colour painted on thickly, opaque acrylic: a yellow-painted wooden house with a big garden behind it, bigger than the other gardens; cucumbers, potatoes, and tomatoes. I am surprised at the tomatoes, and also that the paint on the house is shining. As if Mother were painted out, there's a water butt in the place where she stood in the photo. On the narrow path in front of the house stands a red baby-walker, as if fallen out of time; but why not, why shouldn't there be a baby-walker standing here. I don't see any children, or any other toys. I step near the fence but don't dare enter the garden and I wonder if I should call out; perhaps there is someone there. Suddenly I smell the smoke of burning herbs, stronger than before and as I look in one of the windows, I believe I see a face. I hear a murmuring, begging words, I don't dare to turn around, the voice comes nearer, close to my ear, I feel a breath from behind as the smell of herbal smoke intensifies; I can scarcely breathe and, as I look down, I see my arms empty.

The train has stopped. The compartment door is open; at the other end of the carriage there are raised voices. Maja presses Anja to her, holding her tight; she lays a hand on her head. Anja rubs her lips with her little fists without waking up.